barcode

barcode

bar stories

Pure Slush Vol. 8

Pure
Slush

barcode *Pure Slush Vol. 8* is edited by Matt Potter
and published by Pure Slush, August 2013.

Front cover photograph:
a bar right off Spring Garden in Philadelphia, August 2009
copyright of Andrew T. Marx, Philadelphia, USA.

ISBN: 978-1-925101-00-3

You can find *Pure Slush* at http://pureslush.webs.com

View and purchase all *Pure Slush* books and eBooks
at http://pureslush.webs.com/store.htm

All queries re *Pure Slush* can be made via email to edpureslush@live.com.au

A note on punctuation and spelling

Pure Slush proudly features (both online and in print) writers from all over the English-speaking world. Some speak and write English as their first language, while for others, it's their second or third or even fourth language. Naturally, across all versions of English, there are differences in punctuation, spelling and meaning. These differences are reflected in the stories *Pure Slush* publishes, and accounts for any differences in punctuation, spelling and meaning found within these pages.

stories by

Christopher Allen

Claudia Bierschenk

Arthur Carey

Jennifer Chardon

Ramon Collins

Paul Combs

Norman Conquest

Christine Cook

Joanna Delooze

Shane Frazier

S. H. Gall

Gloria Garfunkel

Walter Giersbach

Teresa Burns Gunther

Kyle Hemmings

Joanne Jagoda

Joyce Juzwik

Len Kuntz

Matt McGee

Matt Potter

Misti Rainwater-Lites

Stephen V. Ramey

Martha Rand

Desmond Shortt

Beate Sigriddaughter

Karen Eileen Sikola

Andrew J. Stone

Ben Tanzer

Alun Williams

Diana J. Wynne

for

'Suzon'

Preface

There's something wonderfully sleazy – and levelling – about bars and bar stories. They certainly don't *have* to be sleazy – just read many of the stories in these pages – but there's always the possibility that a bit of alcohol and some smoking and hair let down and belts loosened can lead to candour and laughter and exposé.

barcode (the idea) was originally an anthology of connected stories set in a UK book shop (and that scenario still appeals) ... but it morphed ... well, really, it *slid* ... into the collection you're now holding in your hands. Perhaps as a reaction to the supposed highbrow (funny, considering!) *Catherine refracted Pure Slush Vol. 7*, I thought hey, maybe we need some earthy counterpoint ...

And what has been great is that many writers sent stories they would not normally submit to *Pure Slush*.

Thanks to those who submitted stories for *barcode*, thanks for reading, thanks to all the bartenders who appear in these stories wiping down a bar, but more importantly, a piece of late night advice: read these stories as if they're a different drink each on the drinks menu. Don't glug them down all in a single session, and give each one the savouring and the contemplation it deserves.

Too much, too soon? No one likes a sloppy drunk!

Now, who's buying the next round?

Matt Potter, editor *Pure Slush*, August 2013

True Shock

by Matt McGee

How many do I know like her?

The bar scene is a tunnel. You go in, you get comfortable. People recognize you, you come back. Regularly. Then daily. Pretty soon you don't remember what the outside world looks like, all you see is the inside of the bars and the mildly good time you're having in an alcohol-coated head.

Then one day, the shock.

Someone dies. Well, a lot of people have died, and most of the time you're so well bunkered into the tunnel you don't feel it. It doesn't bother you until you get home. It's warm and numb and insulated here for now, and your only worry is, 'will there be money enough to pay the tab so I can keep coming back?'

Then, one day – the True Shock.

You wake up in the morning to a voicemail that changes your life forever. Or beside someone you'll have to remember, because the doctor visits have become a lifetime commitment to staying alive. Or sometimes, you don't make it home at all. The police take you into custody because you hit a stalled car with two young kids inside. Still in the tunnel, you ran the kid over a second time while making your getaway.

True Shock comes as a rap on the door in the form of the people who followed you home from the scene.

Horror isn't waking up in a cell, washing with things your family bring you once a week, wearing what the county gives you.

It's when you sit in a room with a lawyer who tells you how many years you'll be staying. It's hearing the child's mother sob in court, even though she isn't trying to. It's a faucet for her now, and you don't know when or if it's ever going to turn off.

It's knowing that this is never who you wanted to be.

And you had enough warning.

Because here I am.

Parasites

by Len Kuntz

Inside the cruise ship cabin it smells like a sewer, hot and humid, air ripe with the stench of fecal matter. Our three year-old daughter lays twisted on the slim cot, head lopped over my wife's lap. Our daughter's hair is matted to her forehead, a sweaty mess. As my wife, Jess, sings 'Rock-a-bye Baby' our daughter moans like a cow about to give birth.

Outside the cabin window, fat-assed rain falls in a slanted torrent. The only nice weather we've had this whole week occurred the first day when we sailed to a remote island. Jess is pretty certain that's where our girl got a parasite even though the water was as clear as glass. The doctor on board said, "You never know," and now we're waiting for her stool sample results.

When I stand, my wife asks where I'm going, same as she always does whether we're a thousand miles at sea or back home.

"I need some air."

My wife glares at me.

"Just a little bit."

As I bend down to kiss our little girl, Jess leans away, and I think that says it all, how we've become untethered.

Atop the ship, I'm soaked in seconds. The trip had been my idea, but now I feel trapped.

I go to one of the boat's restaurants, saddle up to the bar, order Glenlivet neat. After I order another, a woman takes the stool next to mine. She's wearing a tight aquamarine dress with sequins that wink in all directions. My first thought is hooker, but this is a Disney cruise and it's hard to imagine prostitutes picking a place like this to troll for customers.

We make small talk, her initiating it. She's from Jersey, divorced, has a kid who she's left with her ex for the week. She wants to know what my wife looks like, how long we've been together, and without directly asking, she wants to know if it's a happy marriage.

I don't tell her about our sick child, how I found out a year ago that the kid's not even mine, just a bounce back retaliation because of an affair I'd had myself. Instead, I say, "It's all good."

She chuckles breathy, sending up plumes of sweet and sour air. "Come on," she says, "nobody's got it all good."

Her hand is on my thigh now, a warm iron, heavy and light at the same time, and she's leaning in with a wicked smile that says she's dangerous, ready for anything.

I picture my wife in the cruise ship cabin, cradling a sick girl I promised to love as my own. I imagine the heat of the room, the rank odor of my daughter's diarrhea, the claustrophobia, how the cabin walls seem to press inward the more I'm there.

I think about how easy one thing is, how difficult another.

I pay the bar tab, tell the woman goodbye and head back, focused on eliminating every last parasite.

Cabeceo

by Beate Sigriddaughter

A stately woman sat down next to me, gorgeous, silver hair in a crew cut, flowing black skirt, black tunic, and a wine red scarf. She swept into her chair with a delicious scent of lilacs.

"I'm Katherine," she said in an alto voice.

"I'm Robin. Nice to meet you."

We watched the dancers on the floor perform their intricate footwork and cheek-to-cheek tango embraces for half a song. "Do they practice cabeceo here?" she asked.

"I don't know," I confessed. "I've heard of it. What exactly is it?"

"Oh, the man asks the woman to dance from across the room by raising his eyebrows or with a nod of his head, and she accepts with a small nod of her own. Or, if she doesn't want to dance, she simply looks away. If she accepts, he then comes over to formally invite her. And off they go."

"Ah," I said. "What if you don't have perfect vision and vanity makes you not wear glasses?"

"It gets confusing. You might consider contacts. Also, it's best not to sit in front or behind somebody."

She gave me an apologetic look. She happened to sit in front of me at a cafeteria-style table for eight, her chair closest and most convenient to the dance floor.

"And it's best not to sit in a corner or otherwise out of the way. And you must look perky and eager to dance, of course, and preferably not be chatting with your friends." She chuckled in recognition of our obvious sins.

Unfortunately I'd been taught exactly the opposite. I was to appear fully engaged, laughing with my girlfriends, and totally surprised when a man asked me to dance, astonished out of my busy personal life. Who me? Now? But tango was a different religion, it appeared.

Katherine kept speaking, sinning, eyes sparkling, like a connoisseur. Which she was, it turned out. She'd been to Buenos Aires. Twice.

"It's to protect the man's ego. It spares him the embarrassment of rejection. It's just a small gesture that stays between him and the woman. If she doesn't want to dance with him, nobody else ever needs to know."

My youngest nephew came to mind, complaining at the zoo recently how human beings had to eat with knife and fork, no matter how complicated it was, while tigers did not. I wanted to claim just such an injustice here. There was no rule, no codigo, for protecting the women from having to sit at the edge of the dance floor, unclaimed in full view of all.

But we didn't get into that because just then a tall young blond man asked Katherine to dance. She danced well.

I was now closest to the dance floor, wishing for a law that would protect my exposed ego, or else for an excellent dancer to come ask me to dance.

The Man Who Can't be Moved

by Christopher Allen

I met James at The Milk Bar. We didn't actually 'meet' in the social sense of that word and his name's probably not James, but I like the name James. It has the dignity I associate with the man. We hooked up in the bathroom twenty-eight years ago, and then he vanished. Back then The Milk Bar was Buds – without an apostrophe, short for buddies – but everyone called it Butts. Jokes like this were funny in the 80s. Today The Milk Bar is called The Milk Bar.

It's a lesbian bar, and I'm the mascot. Like a badger or a tomahawk or a green dragon. Shay, or Barkeep as she likes to be called, knows everything there is to know about me. I stay glued to the bar except to make my nightly pilgrimage to the restroom – that sacred place to which James will one day return, like a salmon or a Hindu. One night he'll just be there because that's how life works.

"That ain't how life works, Howard." Shay has a way of telling it like it is while rubbing the bar with a damp cloth. Shay has impressive triceps and a tattoo on the right one that says SKUNK.

"I'm nostalgic," I say.

"This is a lesbian bar, Howard. He ain't gonna come here looking for a guy he screwed –"

"Actually, it was the other –"

"– thirty years ago."

"– way around, and it was twenty-eight years ago. He'll come."

A hand clamps down on my spare tire. It's my buddy Echo. He's a year into his transformation and not moody anymore. Echo, whose incredibly inappropriate name used to be Britney, chooses to be called Echo.

"Hey, Buds." I call Echo Buds because we're buds just like the old name of the bar and I'm nostalgic.

"How," Buds says, throwing up a hand like an Indian in the movies.

So here's the thing: Not every night but almost every night, when I shuffle off to the john to commune with James and take a leak, there's a message on the bathroom wall for me. How do I know it's for me? It's a men's restroom at a lesbian bar. I'm the only one who goes in there, except maybe for the person who writes me the message. I get that.

Tonight's message is swirly and big on the wall of the first stall. It says

GET ON WITH YOUR LIFE, HOWARD.

"What does that mean?" I ask Buds when I get back to the bar. He gives me a look like I'm thick.

He's heard my story before, but I still go on about James being my first love and how there's a cosmic connection, planets or something nostalgic like planets that's going to align someday pulling us two back together. I sing the first verse and chorus of The Script's 'The Man Who Can't Be Moved' because – and this is spooky – it comes on the radio while I'm going on about James. My falsetto is not as successful as it could be since I've had four pale ales, but I am that man on the evening news who can't be moved, holding up his cardboard sign with 'Have U seen this girl?' – except mine says 'Have U seen this guy? I don't have a picture, but he's medium height, medium weight, brown-maybe-blonde hair, maybe named James but probably not.'

"Howard," Barkeep says. "It's only a song. Life don't work like that. In real life, you sit on that corner until you're shitting yourself and drinking rubbing alcohol for breakfast. He's gone, Howard. Dead. Or married in Iowa. Or both."

24

I squint at Barkeep. She knows a lot about life and alcohol. But I have this feeling, you know. There was something about James. Not something in the way he moved, like in that James Taylor song or in his looks – I wouldn't know him from Adam today – but something deeper, something like his essence, like I would know his scent or something. Like in that movie 'Perfume'.

Buds has got some peckers with him tonight so we can all help decide which one he's going to purchase. It's nice to be included. My favorite is the big, floppy silicone one, but Buds says he wants a real pecker that gets hard, one he can pump up by squeezing his new balls, which I tell him isn't a pleasant thing to do. The silicone one costs about 30 dollars, and the operation to get a real one costs a thousand times more, and Buds' insurance isn't paying. We start a donation jar, and I put in a starter dollar.

Buds assumes I know my way around a pecker or two, but truth be told James was my first and last love. Since I haven't told anybody this because of the embarrassment aspect, I tell Buds that a limp pecker is lame – although secretly it's still my favorite. It's heavy. But if he's set on getting it up, he needs to make sure everyone on Facebook, Twitter and Kickstarter knows about his donation jar at The Milk Bar.

Then I excuse myself. Where's the loneliest place on earth if it isn't the men's toilet at The Milk Bar? It's so quiet in here, like a church when everyone's gone home, or I guess anyplace when everyone's gone. Doesn't have to be a church.

I check the stalls. Here's another strange thing. The messages are always gone the next day, like someone erases them or like the messages seep back into the cement. I'm not seeing things. I get Buds to come in and confirm the sightings.

Tonight, the message is all the way down the row in the last stall. It says

Redefine Yourself or Your Past Will Define You, Howard.

Preachy, right? Sometimes the messages get up in my face. They all end with Howard, so I can't help taking it personal. I know what this one means. I think everyone's familiar with the Madonna concept. I've tried to redefine myself. I've tried parting my hair on the left, growing a beard and wearing low-rise jeans. So: everything.

I turn off my iPhone and sit here, fingering the message scrawled on the tile wall in the same swirly, big letters as always. I remember the good old days when Buds was the best place in town for playing gay billiards – that's regular pool except with points for looking good bending over the table to shoot – and the best place in the world for feeling loved.

I hum 'Holiday' and wipe my behind. There's a world of wisdom in Madonna songs – except 'Borderline'. I sit here retracing the letters in the message. Maybe I should change my name or get calf implants. Or learn Turkish or go back to junior college. Or pull up stakes and move to Key West. But I can't do that. I have to be here when James comes back.

When I was a boy – tangent time – I used to collect stamps. I wrote to 'Boy's Life' and got that bag of stamps for a dollar plus handling because they all looked so dusty rose and valuable in the picture. But when they arrived, my daddy said the stamp on the envelope from 'Boy's Life' was worth more than all the old stamps in "that stupid bag".

Lying there on my twin bed in a pile of worthless stamps, I taped them in the album anyway. I liked the way they smelled and how they fit into their special places. The feeling I could find something rare made my groin ache. It still does. I don't know why I told you that; it just came to me, so I told it.

There's a certain (creepy) beauty in knowing the writer of these messages knows my name. They could be talking to another Howard – I get that – but I'd like to think someone is talking to me, like I'm worth the time. I trace Howard on the tiles one last time, zip myself up and leave the stall. "iPhone," I say and go back in to get it.

Here's the funny thing: When I look up at the wall, the message is fading right before my eyes. There could be all sorts of explanations for this. Poor quality ink on a less than porous surface comes to mind first. A little man behind the walls sucking the ink through a straw is second. For the life of me I can't think of a third.

5

Sammy the Madman's Near Death Experience

by Walter Giersbach

Sammy the Madman was a self-described existentialist, and was quick to add that he was devoted to exercising his free will in a purposeless universe. While he never acknowledged any needs, he certainly had lots of wants. Since his biggest want was probably a death wish, he should have been glad his wish was unfulfilled so far. His poor wife Sarah certainly was glad because he was the only one bringing home a paycheck.

Sammy was a short, dark, medieval-looking guy in our neighborhood. The Lower East Side of New York City. He should have been an abbot or a monk. Reason I say this is that he always managed to bring up the subject of passing over in general, and specifically the number of near-death experiences he'd had. Then he'd want to discuss the larger picture and put his experiences into a philosophical context.

One night, a bunch of us were considering the merits of the Beatles versus the Beach Boys, and why New Yorkers got mellow when they were stoned while West Coast people just wanted to run and jump in the surf. Everyone asks eternal questions. I'd like to know if my girlfriend's love will last forever. Even Holden Caulfield, who defined my adolescence, asked, "Where do the ducks in Central Park go in the winter?" That's the kind of thing you might want to chat about while sipping a brew at the White Horse in the

Village or up at Pete's Tavern. But then Sammy interjected something from Martin Buber.

That was Sammy. He'd bring up Nietzsche or Bergson or Kant as soon as the barkeep put a glass in front of him. Further, he wouldn't toss off a phrase just to give his point a little depth or some academic *savoir faire*. We could take that, knowing he translated Russian technical manuals for a living and majored in philosophy before being asked to leave Queens College. We could have *ignored* Sammy if he would just let his obscure reference float away over our heads.

But no, he'd drop phrasing on the table like a hammer, and say, "Buber explained it wasn't Eve simply *eating* from the Tree of Knowledge. Adam and Eve didn't have to die after eating the fruit. They just plunged into human mortality."

There would be a stunned silence while people tried to figure how the hell that related to John Lennon's lyrics in 'Let It Be'. Sammy just smiled his wimpy grin.

He didn't mind if Klein the Biker or Allen the Stockbroker told him to knock it off. Everybody ignored Sammy. I didn't tell Sammy off, but neither did I encourage him, because I understood Sammy *always* talked about death. Sammy was on close personal terms with the Grim Reaper, he'd had so many close brushes with death.

But death is not a conversation starter at a party. No one wanted to hear how he once was plunged into a bathtub full of ice to bring down a mortal case of pneumonia. Or how he rode out with his friend who was an ambulance driver and discovered it was his girlfriend's body they dragged from a car wreck. Or about the time he was forced to play Russian roulette with some homeboys in Chelsea. For a quiet guy, Sammy got around.

That evening was one of those times when we had enough. Klein, Allen, Sammy and I were having a few over at this Irish place – O'Neill's on Avenue B – when Klein got really tired of the drift Sammy's conversation was taking. Klein looked like a woolly bear with more hair than a barbershop. I knew he was mad when all I could see were two beady eyes popping out of his furry face.

"Sammy, you are really bringing us down with your morbid talk. Why don't you go home to Sarah and your kid?" he said.

I added, "You're worse than morbid tonight. You'd make an undertaker look like Happy Jack the Clown."

Sammy did his self-effacing grin, like he'd been caught doing something nasty, and he got up. "I have to go to the bathroom," he announced. I guessed he had taken the hint and was bowing out gracefully.

We had a heck of a night. Allen got it in his head that we should do a progressive dinner. We would have one course – and only one course – each at a different place, giving new definition to eating on the run. Allen's a good man for coming up with original ideas.

We finished up at O'Neill's and cabbed down to Mott Street to get some snails at Hong Fat's for an appetizer, then we caught another cab to a Mexican place on Greenwich Avenue for gazpacho, and walked to Delancey for the best pastrami in the city. From there, we went back to Angelo's on Mulberry and Grand Streets for pasta, and down to the Chinese place on Bayard for mango ice cream. New York is the greatest place for turning dining into performance art.

The phone was ringing when I got back to my apartment. It was about 2 a.m. and it was Sammy's wife.

"Jake, I'm looking for Sam. He's not home."

"Sarah? I have no idea where Sam is."

"Isn't he with you now?" she asked in her little-girl New Jersey voice. She pronounced "now" as "na-y-aow," with three syllables. "He said he was going to be with you."

"Yeah, Sarah, he was with us – but that was hours ago. He disappeared while we were sipping a brew."

"I thought you'd take care of him," she said, her voice trailing off. "How could you let him wander off? By himself."

That brought me down. Should we have taken care of him? At 2 a.m. it wasn't a pressing question and I went to sleep. Sammy was a survivor.

Olympics-style eating and drinking can only happen on weekends if you have a straight job during the other five days. That's why it disturbed me every time Sammy said, "Every night is Saturday night for us existentialists." I'll never be an existentialist until I can treat Monday like Saturday. So it was the following

Saturday before I ran into Sammy on Second Avenue. He was studying the posters in the window of the St. Mark's Theatre, probably wondering if he was up to another Orson Welles film.

I said, "Sarah was looking for you last Saturday. She called me at two in the morning. Where'd you go?"

The little smile came over his face.

"I got up to go to the bathroom." He shrugged. "It's kind of a ... story."

I bought us some coffee at Austin's deli and he proceeded to tell me about his disappearance. He said he recalled getting up from the bar and weaving off toward the men's room. He opened the door and that was the last thing he remembered. When he woke up it was dark and he was lying flat on his back. Slowly, he said, he felt around and his fingertips touched walls on all sides of him.

"I thought I must be dead and I'm in my coffin. It was so still and quiet. Not a sound. But then I wondered, if I'm dead, why do I still have to go to the bathroom?

"And I felt around some more and found I was lying on beer cans. I was lying in the box where they throw the empties down in the basement. I took the wrong door to the men's room and fell down the basement stairs."

Feeling the spirit, I exhaled a "Jesus," more to encourage the rest of this story than to lend it theological emphasis.

"Then what happened? We waited for you," I lied.

He shrugged. "Well, I went upstairs. The bar was empty. Everyone had gone. It was locked up. I was locked in. There was nothing I could do, so I sat down at the bar and got a beer."

I began laughing so hard the coffee snorted out my nose.

"Then the cops came and banged on the door, and they called O'Neill, and O'Neill came down and opened up, and the cops arrested me. For breaking and entering. I tried to explain I didn't *break* in, because I was *already* in, and being already in I couldn't enter. You can't go in twice – philosophically speaking – without at least going out once. But they took me down to the 9th Precinct and booked me. I think the judge will give me probation."

I yanked a paper napkin out of the dispenser and dried my eyes.

"Well, Sammy," I said, "you remind me of those immortal words spoken by that profound thinker, Emanuel Kant."

His eyes lit up. I was on his turf now, talking philosophy. "What's that?"

"He said, 'If it's not one thing, it's another.'" I put my hand on his arm and tried to look serious. "The cops booked you for impersonating a philosopher."

6

Mac's Place

by Joanne Jagoda

It was a miserable night. I remember the foghorns and the briny smell of the ocean. Since we are only three blocks from the beach, fog often rolls in like a damp blanket. It was mid-August, but that's how summer can be in San Francisco. Don't expect to go around in shirtsleeves.

My name is Adam Rory McInerney. The patrons of my fine drinking establishment, McInerney's Irish Pub, call me 'Mac'. My father opened this bar in 1938. Everyone called him 'Pop'. I had no intention of winding up here. I went to San Francisco State and studied accounting. It was 1969, and Uncle Sam had other plans for me. I was drafted and sent to Vietnam. Luckily I came home in one piece, but I was lost and aimless. This city was filled with long-haired hippies and anti-war protestors, and I didn't belong anywhere. When Pop had his stroke in 1971, he needed me, and I've been here ever since.

This is a simple place and I'm a simple man. Neighborhood bars like mine are becoming obsolete. My fair city has been overrun by chichi establishments catering to the dot.com hipsters. I make drinks the old-fashioned way, poured and shaken. If you want fancy designer drinks, with infusions of rosemary or girly, fizzy concoctions with umbrellas, go to Chestnut Street or South of Market where they'll charge you $11.50 and you've got my blessing. I pour a stiff drink, charge a fair price, and I'll listen to whatever's on your mind, no charge.

And let me tell you, forty-two years of pouring behind this oak bar with its gouges and welts, I've heard more than a few tales. My regulars are the working stiffs: the UPS drivers, the plumbers, the painting contractors and the construction guys who want a quick one before going home. If there's one thing I've learned, it's that people are full of surprises. The person you pegged as a mean sonofabitch can be a softie, and the one you expect to be a fine upstanding citizen is a low-life. When I retire, which I'm planning next year when I'm sixty-five, I want to write. You wouldn't expect a burly guy like me, all six foot four and two hundred and fifty pounds, to want to sit behind a computer. The last few years, I've been taking writing workshops at City College and I've got lots of stories to get out, maybe even a book.

Here's one of them. It was two years ago tonight. I had told Mattie she could have the night off. It was just me and Del my other cocktail waitress which was OK since Wednesdays are slow. Four guys were playing pool. A few people were at tables watching a Giants game on the big screen TV; a couple of guys were sitting at the bar. I was wiping down the counter when the door tinkled and she walked in.

Mind you we get our share of ladies here with their boyfriends or sometimes a gaggle will come in for a drink after work. But I'd never seen the likes of her. She was a looker; in her thirties, tall, in a midnight blue evening gown draped over her body like she was a movie star, high-heeled silver sandals, and red painted toes. She didn't care that her dress dragged on the sawdust floor, but I recall that didn't sit right with me. She had a fur shrug over her shoulders. Everyone stopped what they were doing and stared, including me. I was sure she'd want a drink with an umbrella, but she asked for a scotch by brand, just one word.

"Dewars," she said in a raspy voice like she'd been crying. Then she hoisted her bum on one of the leather stools. She gnawed on the cuticle of her thumbnail.

"Yes ma-am. Coming right up. Neat or on the rocks?"

"No ice."

I poured her two fingers and placed the drink in front of her. After a minute the other patrons lost interest and you could hear the pool balls clacking and shouts about the Giants.

She finished her drink in three big swallows, grimaced, then held the glass out.

"Ma-am, if you don't mind my saying so, you seem a bit out of place here. Is there some way I could help you?"

I filled her glass again though I knew it was a bad idea.

This one she drank slower, closed her eyes and exhaled long and slow. Her face relaxed for a few seconds. She really was a beauty – porcelain complexion, short black hair, a dusting of cinnamon freckles on her nose, long dark lashes, and when she opened her eyes they were a bluish-gray, like the ocean.

A shadow crossed her face. "Do you want something?"

I was flustered which never happens to me. She made me feel like a bug she could mash under her heels. "Oh, sorry, Miss. I didn't mean to be in your face."

A tear rolled down her cheek. She shook her head. "I didn't mean to sound like a bitch."

I kept wiping the bar.

"I shouldn't have told him tonight."

I started on drying the wet shot glasses.

"I'm leaving him," she continued. "I'm in love with someone else. She's the best thing that's ever happened to me. I met her at the gym. I didn't plan to tell him tonight at the symphony opening but he started a fight because his tux wasn't pressed correctly and I lost it. I couldn't take it anymore. Ten years with him and I could never please him … not even get his goddamn suit done right. He beats on me with his words. You can't see the damage outside but inside I'm black and blue."

Whoa. I didn't expect to hear this … or maybe I did.

"He didn't raise his voice … just whispered, 'I'm taking the children away. You'll never see them again.'" More tears spilled from her eyes, darkening them like clouds before a storm.

I handed her napkins. "That's rough but he might come around. Miss, you need to find a good attorney."

She laughed bitterly. "He *is* an attorney … one of the city's biggest firms and very rich. He can get what he wants. I'll never see my babies." She sniffled, reached in her evening bag, threw $20 on the bar and slid off her stool. I stood there watching her gown trail in the sawdust as she walked out.

Del came over. "Whoa, that was intense."

"Yeah, well she's got some big stuff on her mind."

"Oh those rich chicks, they don't have nothing to worry about, just getting their nails done. She'll get over it ..."

I hoped Del was right. Then I got busy with a group of rowdy guys who came in to watch the Giants game, but she stayed in my head gnawing at me. There was a sadness about her that no words could fix.

I closed up at 2:30am, drove home and was greeted at the door by Roger, my French bulldog. He was waiting for his nuzzle then sauntered back to his spot on the floor and was snoring in seconds. I poured myself a bowl of Cheerios which I eat every night when I get home. Sitting in my recliner, I kept seeing her dress dragging in the sawdust.

I should have followed her.

I fell asleep brooding in my chair and didn't get up until ten.

I went in to work early. I was putting change in the register and heard the door rattle. It was around 3:45, too early for Del and Mattie. I looked up and saw Jimmy Larkin. Officer James Larkin is a second-generation cop. I knew his dad.

"Hey, Mac."

"Hey, Jimmy. Ya' want a beer?"

"No thanks. I'm on duty. Mac, the body of a young woman washed up on Seal Rock this morning. Found her fur wrap and bag on the sand. She had a napkin from *McInerney's*. Was she here last night?"

I shuddered.

The funeral was a Tuesday. I sat in the back. I should have told her husband I was the last person she spoke with but part of me wanted to punch him out. I owed it to her.

On nights like this when I hear the foghorns I think she is calling to me for help. I've got to write down this story about that night, but I'm going to give her a different ending. Maybe then I can put this behind me.

7

Plonk

by Teresa Burns Gunther
with apologies to Jamaica Kincaid

First thing you come in, get busy cleaning up this dog's breakfast. If those galahs from the night before didn't take out the rubbish, do that first. Wash the leftover glasses and hang them up here to dry, don't break 'em, we go through 'em fast enough on a good night. If you got the time, rub the lips off the rims. Sweep the floor – what? No, just push it out the effing door. Tell Sammy to boil beets if the arsehole forgets again; rub 'em out of their skins; no, let them cool first, and mind your clothes! The buggers stain, chop them beets, but not too small – like this – or they make an effin mess, slop in some salad cream, yeah Brit Mayo, and whatnot. Chop the onions if Sammy's off his face, get the bangers from the freezer, bung 'em in the fridge here. You're a vejjo? Bloody wombat! Suit yourself, but have your tucker before we open – Fridays and Saturday nights are screamers, you won't have time once the Bobby Moore's open. You can drink as much as you bloody well like but don't waste the wine, you hear me? And I don't want to see you giving it away free to some bloke you got hotties for. *I won't, I'm no thief, does it matter which wine I drink?* You drink the plonk, the cleanskins; the fancy's for the paying customers; this is how to work the cash register – you know how to make change, Yank? Okay. Watch your tips, put 'em quick under the bar; these animals will steal your gran's teeth. Wear something light, it gets hot as hell in here, make sure it's tight and show some titty, you ever seen a bloke behind this bar? There's the reason. And don't be a bludger, this is how you open the plonk –

you Yanks don't have this supreme gadget, still using handheld ones like it means something; open twenty of each, bang the corks back in, stack reds here, slap the whites on the ice, but nab the corks when you sell 'em – the more these yobbos spill, the more we sell, besides we'll need the corkers for later. You'll see. You know how to work a grill? Right, see this is how you turn it on, steaks on first, bangers second – not too fast or they explode. If they do, jam 'em in a bun. What's that? Nah, no worries, we keep the lights low. Smile, even at the arseholes, but if they come over the bar, yell for Jimmy. I'll come runnin'. If I don't, this's where I keep me bat. Slap it, like this, once – coppers say we're s'posed to give a warning – stand big as you can, not so easy for a little thing like you, so wear high heels, anyone comes over my bar, smack him, the other fools will love you for it, tip ya', buy ya' grog. If the coppers ever show, make nice, offer dinner but don't burn theirs, just spit on it when they're not lookin'. Ha! Feed the musician, don't pay him 'til after his second set, he gets dinner, drink and 20 quid a night, but cut off his grog if he stops playin'. Don't let anyone think you're not tough. Be friendly, flirt, but hanky-panky you do on your own time. Jasmine's your partner in crime tonight, she knows the ropes; any questions, ask her. This is how to spot an arsehole, this is how to spot a thief – never deliver goods without the money's in your hand first. This is the signal for trouble; if it's fire, grab the hose, wash everybody down. This is how to serve the salads, this is how to serve the beans; this here's the stout, the lager. You know your white and tan? Good, here's the way you love Guinness into her glass. We close at two, sweep 'em all out, collect the glasses and bottles, hose down the floor, get the chunkies washed out, don't leave it overnight. Lock the doors fast; empty the glasses and bottles: white wine through this funnel, the cab savs and shyraz in that, if you fuck it up – red in the white – start a new white bucket. We'll have some rosé tomorrow, Ha! *But why do I sort the old wine?* Haven't you heard a word I'm sayin'? After all I've been telling you, after all the nights you've been in here drinkin', you don't get the secret of Jimmy's Wine Bar's success? It's the famous house wine. Yeah! Now you get it. Don't make that face, it's the wine that keeps this ship afloat. But don't you tell nobody. When you leave, you girls walk out together, if you're the last, get me – or Sammy if he's still standing – to walk witcha to the station, never hang about after work alone, we've had enough of that kind a sorrow. Yeah, yeah, let's go ...

8

Capitalist Bastard

by Matt Potter

"Ooooo," Peter says, "this is where it gets exciting." He licks his lips, looks at me, and then with a flourish of his wrist, flips it over.

And then – he can't help it, he HAS to do it – looks at Digby.

"It's exciting," he says to Digby, as if to confirm what he's just said to me is true. "Ooo, this is fabulous." He looks at Digby again. "What do you think?"

"Oh, that *is* fabulous," Digby says. "You're right there. Especially that one," and he points to a swatch of grey-mauve velvet shot with silver thread.

"Yes, that's what I was thinking," and Peter nods. "But which section?"

"Oh, the gay one, I was thinking," Digby says.

"Yeah, me too."

"So what section's the gay one?" I ask. (Really, I may as well not be here.)

I sit on an old white wooden chair in the middle of the room, tatty white curtains shielding us from the street on the other side of the window, while they orgasm over a book of fabric samples. Day 3 of paying rent on this place and decisions need to be made.

"'Cause I thought it was supposed to all be mixed together," I continue. And still sitting in the chair, I plant my feet on the floor, glue my hips to the seat, and wave my arms around like a Mixmaster.

"It's about compromise, Alistair," Peter says, no hint of worry in his voice that I might have fallen off the chair and dented the floorboards with a newly-broken pelvis. "Oh my, this is drooolworthy," he adds, stroking a lime green and strawberry velvet shot with gold. "Maybe this can be for the gay part and the grey-mauve can be for the grunge part."

"But grey-mauve isn't very grungey," I say.

"It's not?" Peter asks, not even looking over at me.

"No, it's not really," Digby says, who *is* looking over at me now, if only for a split second. "It's not really grungey at all."

"No," says Peter, "I guess it's more granny-grunge."

"We really need to go back to our original concept," I say, standing up. "We need to revisit that. Right now. Because this is a real crossroads moment here."

"You think?" asks Peter. "Again?" But of course, he's not looking at me, he's looking at Digby still.

"Yes," I say, "I *do* think." And then add, "Again." I look down and kick a piece of wood, some offcut from a previous re-fit, across the floor. It ricochets off the skirting board and spindles into a pile of dust. Hands on my hips, I glare at them.

(I thought this whole venture would be a cute way for Peter – my boyfriend of six months – and Digby – my best friend of six years – to get to know each other better. Ha!)

Peter turns back to the sample book and flips through to the next fabric.

Digby half-smiles and puts his hands on his hips too. "Okay, Alistair, so let's revisit it."

His stance mirroring mine sort of undoes me, and the breath I've been holding escapes me in a big rush so I look like a deflated wine cask bladder. "Well, obviously it's not exactly the same," I say, pausing, breathing in through my teeth, sort of whistling, maybe.

"But your idea was a bit crap really, wasn't it?" Peter says. "I mean, a cake shop in the middle of Berlin?"

"Yeah," I add, "smack bang in the middle of a nation of people obsessed with cake."

"So it's good this idea *is* going to work," Peter says. Looking at Digby again.

I, for one, do not think a cake shop in Schöneberg (the heart of middle class inner-city Berlin, Germany) transplanted into the side streets of West Richmond (the heart of semi-industrial western suburbs Adelaide, Australia) and morphed into a gay-grunge-dessert bar, has quite the same cachet. For a start, the business next door is a plumbing supply depot. In Schöneberg, the business next door would have been a women's clothing shop. Customers could have bought a designer dress from *Lotte Kaumeyer Exclusiv Kreations*, and then walked next door for cake. Here they can go shopping for PVC piping and if they're gay and like dessert, they can walk next door for a frayed-edged custard slice.

The grunge bit?

"It's a genre," Peter had said, "isn't it, Digby?"

"Yes, grunge isn't a style," said Digby, despite my insisting it is a style and not a genre. Despite the fact it's my own mid-life-crisis-so-I-took-very-early-retirement-and-cashed-in-my-savings-to-travel-the-world money paying for this gay-grunge-dessert bar fit-out. Despite the fact ... well ... despite a lot of things.

I even lucked out on the name. I wanted Ganache Panache. Peter said, "I think Insensate is much better. What do you think Digby?"

And Digby said, "Yes, Insensate will be a lot more appealing to the western suburbs light industrial scene-queens."

"Yeah," said Peter. "Insensate is just gayer."

And even then I'd stood up, hands on my hips. "We really need to go back to our original concept," I'd said. "Because this is a real crossroads moment here."

And Peter just laughed and said, "No plumber's going to know what a ganache is. They won't even know what a fruit flange is."

Peter turns away from me. His jeans – tight at the hips, sculpted across the butt, pouchy in just the right lazy, lackadaisical kind of way in the crotch – are stitched with bright yellow thread. It's the first time I've noticed this.

I can't hear what he's saying with his face turned away from me, and neither can Digby, but Digby is closer so he shifts his weight from his right hip to his left. Their hips are millimetres apart now. And Digby's jeans are stitched with yellow thread too.

Digby says something to Peter – I can't hear what but I know it's something because it rustles up a slight breeze in the airless room – and Peter throws his head back (I can see the scalp peering through his thinning crown) and laughs.

"That's enough!" I say, and their heads snap around to look at me. They see me standing with my hands on my hips again, eyes wide and nostrils flaring. "That's enough laughing. How can you laugh and choose fabric at the same time?!"

Digby raises his eyebrows at me, like he thinks I'm about to explode.

"You CAN'T!" I explode, my voice roiling across the ceiling. "You had to turn around and look at me before you could raise your eyebrows!"

"We're not raising our eyebrows, Alistair," says Peter, his voice icy, lips drawn in a pale sneer. "We're choosing fabric for the toilet seat covers."

"Oh," I say. And not knowing what else to say, I say "Oh," again. Then rock back on my heels like I've been blown over.

Peter shakes his head. He smiles at Digby, like he's caught me reading under the covers by torch twenty minutes after my bedtime.

Turning my head, I glance at Peter, out of the corner of my eye, then look at the door.

And in a split second he's stroking my arm, standing beside me so I smell his musky cologne. "I think you're being just a little bit silly, Baba," he coos. (As in Ali Baba. As in Alistair Baba.) And tapping his open palm on my chest, I fall back into the old white wooden chair. He plants a kiss on my forehead. "Your natural paranoia is getting the better of you again."

I sigh and hang my head. Perhaps he's right. The toilet seat covers were my idea. A dumb idea, I know, but they're the only idea Peter and Digby thought was good, so I pushed it. "So you're thinking of gay toilets and grunge toilets and toilets for people who come in for dessert?" I ask, my voice just above a whisper, all measured reason. "Like a toilet trifecta?"

"Yes," Peter says. "I thought that was what you wanted."

I shrug my shoulders. "Yeah, well, I thought that's what *you* wanted," I say. "I'm just being agreeable." I sink against the backrest as Peter and Digby turn back to the sample book.

"You really need to stop being so jealous of us getting along so well," says Digby over his shoulder. "It's *better* that we all get along." And he turns and looks me in the face again. "Isn't it, Baba?"

He's never called me that before, and half-smiling, I nod.

"And anyway," says Peter – and then he stops, just as he hauls one fabric book out of the way and Digby dumps another in its place, their pert yellow-seamed arses in perfect right-to-left unison again – "what's a quick hand job between workmates?"

9

Another Saturday Night

by Stephen V. Ramey

Another rocking Saturday night at the bar. 'Jailbreak' pounds from the jukebox. In the corner, Larceny and Theft writhe through their lezzy rendition. I wipe down a couple of beer stains on the counter that resemble handcuffs.

Theft bends over, toned legs pumping below ragged cutoff jeans. "Tease," Larceny giggles. She tugs her tube top until her breasts are on the verge of their own jailbreak. She doesn't have Theft's legs but she does have nice tits.

Domestic Violence motions from his stool. "You think they're available?" I sense the winding spring of his anticipation.

"Have a beer," I say. "On the house." If I keep him lubricated just right, he'll stay under the radar. Let him tip into drunkenness or sobriety and he can be one bar-smasher of a bad patron.

I pop a bottle top. Domestic turns back to me. "Never say no to free."

A geeky guy peels off the dance floor and strides toward the girls. I sigh. Once Harassment gets involved, you can count on a long night. Indecent Exposure looks over from his perch by the window. I nod toward Harassment. Indy is the only regular who gets along with him.

The jukebox goes dead, amputating Phil Lynott's lyrics. "That was so petty!" Theft says. "How much copper can it be?" The girls slink toward the exit, the severed jukebox cord dragging from Larceny's pant leg like a tail.

Indy intercepts Harassment, and flaps his raincoat like an eagle fanning its nest. "One count," Harassment says. "Two counts, three, four ..." The tip of his pen ticks against that little notebook he always carries around. Indy flashes his electric grin.

"You ready for another beer?" I ask Domestic.

His face balls up for a heartbeat. He watches the girls leave. "On the house?" he says hopefully.

10

A Man Walks into a Barcode

by Norman Conquest

A man walks into a barcode where a bald, bespeckled Irishman in a white lab coat is dusting a circuit board.

"What'll it be?"

"Scotch on the rocks," replies the man.

"Is that for you or your friend?"

"Friend?"

"The woodchuck. On your shoulder."

The man examines his shoulders. "Well, I don't have a woodchu –"

"Doesn't matter, we don't serve liquor here. Try the hotel next door." He chuckles. "Even a woodchuck couldn't miss it."

According to a sign in the lobby the Hotel L'Archipel was hosting the gala annual ISBN convention.

The man asks a bellhop directions and then makes his way to the ballroom entrance. The door is shut and a woman with purple hair, seated at a card table, informs him he will not be admitted.

"I left my tie in the cab," he offers.

The woman shakes her head stiffly. "Sorry, no woodchucks allowed."

The man looks around. He even brushes at his shoulders to be safe. "I don't know what you're seeing, madam, but I –"

"Please check it at the front desk."

The man looks bewildered. He sighs, shakes his head, turns and mumbles, "This is crazy ..."

"Rules are rules," she sniffs.

At the front desk a clerk is busy attending to a young couple checking in. The man glances at his watch, then turns and strides determinedly back to the ballroom entrance.

"That's better," says the purple-haired woman, smiling now. She grabs his hand and rubber-stamps a 13-digit number just below the knuckles. "Go right in."

The Ballroom is immense and filled to capacity. A hundred couples are gyrating to a dance band off in the distance. The musicians are either dressed as snowmen or wearing white tuxedos. He notices to his left a pretty young woman in a pale blue dress, standing alone, holding an empty plastic cup in both hands.

"Excuse me, could you tell me where the bar is?"

She frowns, waves a hand dismissively behind her. "There's no bar," she says, "just a goddam punch bowl. Here" – she hands him her cup – "go ahead, smell it. It's *awful*. Orangey-Kool-Aid or something."

He bends his head ... stares into the cup for a long moment, but doesn't sniff it. He straightens up, glances at a long line of people waiting.

"I'll probably die of thirst in that line," he says.

The woman snorts and flares her nostrils.

"Should've gotten here earlier," she says and walks off.

He nods, shrugs, looks for a place to discard the cup, crumples it and stuffs it in his pocket.

He walks over and takes his place at the end of the line.

'I should have brought a book,' he thinks.

Long after midnight, when they dim the lights, he's still standing there.

Now, sadly, a year later, he's waiting in the punch line.

As for the woodchuck, he abandoned the cloakroom at the first opportunity.

Miracles

by Misti Rainwater-Lites

It was Christmas Eve and she didn't care about such things but she was supposed to care because she was a mother. The boy was with her parents. She was at the bar looking at herself in the mirror as she downed her third Jack & Coke and smoked her third cigarette. She thought she looked good for forty. 'Ten Years of This' by Gary Stewart played on the jukebox. "Kill me and get it over with so I can wake up on a bar stool beside Saint Gary," she said to no one. Then she felt someone standing behind her. She turned around and saw him, whoever the fuck he was. He was tall and skinny in a black t-shirt and blue jeans. He had curly brown hair and a wicked smile.

"Your boyfriend is in the bathroom, right? No way you're here alone," the man said.

"My husband is in the ground. I'm never alone. He fuckin' haunts me," she said. She turned back around and drained her drink. She lit another cigarette and pretended not to notice when he sat down beside her. He ordered a beer. She saw him checking her out in the mirror.

"I'm sorry about your husband," he said.

"Like hell you are."

"My name's Charles. What's yours?"

"Joan Jett."

"You're much more beautiful than Joan Jett. Come on. Let's be friends. It's Christmas Eve. Expect miracles."

"Yeah, okay. Santa will walk through that door any second now and hand me a bright and shiny brand-new life. My name is Lisa. I have a son who is seven years old. He lives with my parents because I'm too much of a fuck-up to take care of him. I have more issues than *Playboy*. If you're lookin' for easy pussy check out those hot chicks hangin' out by the pool tables. They're beggin' for Christmas dick. I'm content to sit here with my good friends Jack Daniels and Gary Stewart."

"Damn. I guess you told me."

"I guess I did."

"I still like you."

"Then you're an idiot."

Lisa ordered another Jack & Coke. She liked the way Charles looked and sounded and smelled. She could see herself riding his dick. But she wouldn't just give him her pussy. She would make him work for it. He was drinking his beer and laughing. Lisa guessed that he didn't get turned down too often.

"Christmas dick, huh? What do you have against Christmas dick?" Charles asked.

"It's against my religion. A lot of things are against my religion. If I suck Christmas dick, drink light beer, listen to top forty trash and watch television I will spend an eternity in Wal-Mart without a dime to my name, surrounded by bawling babies and rednecks with fat asses who keep bumping into me with their carts, filled with Cheetos and honey buns."

"Jesus! Let me pay your tab and take you out for whatever it is you're hungry for."

"What's your favorite movie?"

"'Key Largo.'"

"What's your favorite album to fuck to?"

"'Trout Mask Replica.'"

"What's your sun sign? Don't tell me. You're a Leo."

"I'm a Taurus with Leo rising and a Gemini moon."

"Of course you are. Do you have any sexually transmitted diseases?"

"No ma'am. How about yourself?"

"Clean as a goddamn whistle. Do you have any tattoos?"

"One. A bull on my left arm."

"I've got six tattoos. A rose on my left tit, a cherry on my right hip, a mermaid on my left arm, a tiger on my right arm, a dolphin on my left ankle and barbed wire around my right ankle."

"I don't believe you. Show me."

"I don't have to prove jack shit to you. You just want to get me into bed. You just want to fuck me until I forget who and where I am. I know your kind."

"You haven't been fucked in a while. Is fucking someone until you forget who and where you are such a bad idea?"

"It's the best idea I've heard all night, Charles. But you need more beer. You're much too uptight."

"You're killin' me, darlin'."

He was too drunk to drive his truck and she was too drunk to drive her piece of shit Kia Spectra so he called a taxi. She held onto him in the parking lot and they kissed. She shivered so he took off his black leather jacket and placed it around her shoulders. In the taxi he reached for her hand and raised it to his lips. She crossed her legs and looked out the window at all the lights. There were tears in her eyes. She blinked them away. Goddamn holidays. Presents. Guilt. Expectations. All the pretty lights.

"Damn. This is a nice room," Lisa said. She opened the mini refrigerator and pulled out a bottle of water. She sat on the edge of the king-size bed and drank.

"I've got this room until New Year's. You're welcome to stay with me." Charles sat down beside Lisa and began kneading her back with his hands. Lisa closed her eyes. She'd had affairs since Luke died in the tornado two years ago. But she hadn't cared for any of the men, never had the desire to see any of them more than a couple of times. She already liked Charles too much.

"Goddamn it," Lisa muttered.

"Why are you so angry, baby?" Charles asked.

"Because I like you. I like how you're making me feel. I don't want to like you. I don't deserve any of this."

"You think you deserve less? Tell me what you think you deserve."

"It isn't about deserving. It's about needing. I don't deserve this but I need this. Just fuck me. I need you to fuck me."

They fucked and it was so good that Lisa cried. Charles kissed her wet eyes and wrapped his arms around her. The room was dark and strange but Lisa felt like she was home. She trusted him completely so she fell asleep in his arms. She fell asleep feeling like a baby. Innocent, protected, loved beyond reason. The hard thoughts and negativity disappeared. The hurt went into hiding. The pain had become the biggest part of who Lisa was but for the moment she experienced a sweet reprieve. She was alive and it felt good.

In the morning Lisa opened her eyes. She looked at Charles sleeping beside her. God, he was gorgeous. She wanted to kiss him and snuggle in his arms. But then she thought of her son and the pain returned like an elephant like all of Africa like a planet on her shoulders. Lisa rubbed her eyes and told herself not to cry. Crying was not allowed. She turned on her cheap cell phone and listened to the angry messages from her mother and siblings. They had expected her. It was a tradition in her family. It didn't matter how much you hated each other the rest of the year. You were expected to show up at the parents' house on Christmas Eve for turkey and presents. "Curtis is seven years old, Lisa. It's bad enough that his dad is dead and his mom doesn't have her shit together enough to raise him. You have to screw him over on Christmas Eve, too? God, you're pathetic. Don't bother coming by tomorrow. No one wants to see your sorry ass," Amber said in the message. Amber was Lisa's younger sister, a successful real estate agent with a successful divorce attorney husband named Brett and two beautiful children named Audrey and Alexis. Lisa deleted Amber's message. The next message was from her brother Mitch. He slurred his words in drunken hatred. "You're trash, Lisa. Hope whatever you're doing right now is worth the hell you put your son through. When are you going to grow the fuck up and be a decent mother to my nephew?" Mitch went from job to job and woman to woman. Lisa had loathed him since they were children. He had always been a self-righteous brat with a big mouth and a bad attitude. Lisa deleted the message. The last message was from her mother. Lisa deleted it without listening to it. She wiped away the tears and held her head in her hands.

"Are you okay?" Charles asked from the other side of the bed.

"No. I'm sober," Lisa said.

"Call room service. Order a bottle of champagne. Merry Christmas, sweetness."

He reached for her and they were both naked and warm and the bed was big and it belonged to them until January 1, 2004 and there would be champagne and those were miracles enough for one lifetime. Lisa was tired of crying so she laughed. The laughter felt better.

12

Beaver Lodge

by Desmond Shortt

I never had much to do with beavers. Typical badger me. But about ten years ago half this place was wiped out by roadworks. I had to make some new tracks.

So one morning, I was on my way home. There where the stream bends, I stopped to get my bearings. And a beaver is ducking into a hole. I was curious.

Beavers, they don't mess about. Not like a squirrel. Or a fox. With beavers it's either work or family. And this didn't look like either. Too far from the water. Just a burrow, but in the wrong place.

So I stick my head in. A whole barroom was laid out in there. And not coiled around a tree root like it was laid out by some rodent: a proper long bar with beams and struts. Hand it to beavers: they know how to build.

I slipped in as if there's nothing unusual, joined a few beavers at the bar. They're all sitting in ones or twos. Not a sound out of any of them. And a pool table down the back. It was quiet. Apart from the sports. Night shift finished. Or the morning shift starting. I don't know.

Anyway, it was quiet. But that's how I like it. I'm a badger. What can I say. I ordered a drink. The guy brought it over. Silence. Half an hour passes. Then the place clears out and I do too. And that's how it went for me then, every morning for a few weeks. Like a routine. I'd call in there on the way home, nurse a beer. No one says a word. To me, or anyone else for that matter.

My wife used to ask what I was going in there for. Aren't they different? Won't people talk? What if they rush you? But then, she doesn't think weasels are mammals. I did a little research. Don't ever be afraid to learn a few things. Especially if you are going 'cross the species line.

Can save you the world of trouble. You breathe up a horse's nostrils: you have a friend. Breathe into a cat's: you'll be eating your breakfast through the side of your face. Beavers: industrious, monogamous, family values, nocturnal. They're just like badgers. But without all the biting. A badger bar? Can't see that happening.

About five weeks I had been going in. It was like my routine, on the way home. Then one morning I go in, sit down. Guy brings me a beer (without even asking at this stage), I look around. Every beaver in the place is standing in a line beside me along the bar. I didn't know which way to look.

The bartender comes out. And he introduces them all to me, one after the other; Billy Beaver, Bobby Beaver, Barry Beaver. Well they all look the same to me: no stripe. But I go along anyway. "Hello, hello, hello." It was like ... acceptance. Like I'd passed the test. And the next morning it's all, "Hey Badger. Hi Badger. Top o' the morning Badger!"

So I stopped going in after that.

13

WTF?

by Shane Frazier

Randy opens the door to Money Plays, and steps in, eyes in momentary darkness while he adjusts to the shadowy interior. The end of 'Superman Lover' plays over the speakers, JGW's guitar riffs flowing through the bar in waves. Like he's casing the joint, he scans the scene, looking for his quarry. But at 2:35 on a Tuesday, the place is almost empty. Only Stan-stan the Bartender Man – unloading a case of Full Sail – is visible. No target. So he isn't even here? Half-black muthafucker. Beat his ass when I see him.

Looking up, Stan-stan steps to the bar's edge and extends his large hand in greeting. "Mister Moore. My man. Been a minute. What can I get you sir?"

Randy scowls as he half-heartedly shakes the owner's hand. Scanning the bar again, just to make sure, he breathes out and says without looking at Stan-stan, "Can I have a Heineken? And have you seen Jason? He's supposed to meet me here."

Stan-stan turns to a frost-covered spigot, pours Randy's drink. "I haven't seen him in a few. I heard from Lanni that you were goin' to drop in. Something about an incident that happened a few days ago? Last week?" Stan-stan slides the beer in front of his patron, feigning concern with a furrowed brow.

Lanni knows? Shit. She knows, so everyone knows. And that's how Stan-stan knows. Shit.

Randy picks up the beer and drinks deep, emptying half of the bottle. 'Superman Lover' ends as the Stones' 'Satisfaction' begins. Setting the bottle down with a large wood-glass thump, Randy looks back at Stan-stan. Stan-stan smiles a half-smile, almost as if he timed the song to fit the moment. Looking him up and down, he stops. Mistake. That black man would destroy you, idiot. You see his shoulders. What do you think is making that Ruckus shirt fit so tight, soft-ass living?

Stan-stan reaches under the bar and takes out a folded piece of paper. "Lanni handed it to me this morning, before she left. I assumed she talked to you. She said it's from Jason."

Randy opens the paper and reads the letter.

April 3, 2012

Randy;

WTF??? This is how we are goin' to handle this? Seriously? Just so we are clear, let me give you the truth on how this went down. If you insist on feeling this way, then at least you will have the facts.

Last week, when Maria and I went to the bar, Tracy was already there, and had a few too many (according to Stan-stan the Bartender Man). We sat next to her, and caught up since it had been months since we had spoken. It was a few hours before anything was even brought up (and it was Tracy who brought this shit up in the first place). There was no conversation, or attempts at making 'this happen'; it really was just a spur of the moment thing. You are making an effort to color this in a 'we went there knowing she was there and having a plan', and that simply isn't accurate. In fact, it is downright a lie.

I know you are heated in this, but I do believe that your anger is misdirected, homey! And while I understand that this is a hold-out from 20 years ago (your pisstivity), again, it is misplaced. We are all adults, and all of us (save you) have acted accordingly. Tracy is still a 37 year-old woman who can think for herself, and you coming to defend her is admirable, but unnecessary. She was never in danger, and she made an adult choice. Sorry dude, but I think you have to live with this.

That is it. That is how it went down. Again, this is not how I want to resolve this, since I feel that there is nothing to resolve. But you not talking my calls is just petty and bitch-mode, and you know this. Answer my damn phone call, and stop being shitty just because my wife and I fucked your sister.

Peace & Smoke homey ...

J

So Different Now

by Ben Tanzer

She's right there in Thirsty's. In her usual spot. Drinking her usual drink. Yuengling on tap. One after another.

And he's there too. Behind the bar. Pouring drinks. One after another.

Sometimes they speak. But mostly she orders. He pours. And so it goes.

The three of us, Becky, Jamie and me, went to MacArthur elementary school together. MacArthur was built on top of a swamp and now allegedly sinks one millimeter into the ground every year, year in and year out. Of course, maybe that's just the local folklore.

Becky had lived over by St. Johns Church, near Mill Hill. Her older brother Billy was a famous high school drunk. Her dad had died when we were all young – it was something on a construction site – and after that Becky's mom always looked a little confused, her eyes dreamy, and her focus somewhere else.

Becky was on her own from the start. She got herself up for school. Got dinner made and even paid the bills when needed.

She also followed me around. At first it was just around school, moving desks to be closer to me, maybe changing tables in the lunchroom. It was harmless. But then I started seeing her as I was leaving school. Drifting across the lawn, watching me, following me with her eyes, and then every day, venturing just that much further, up the hill in front of school and towards the crosswalk and the crossing guard, the one who had lost her nose to cancer and now wore this triangle thing in the spot where her nose had been.

And then she walked past the crosswalk and the creepy house where the old shut-in lady lived, the one who waved to me as I walked to and from school even as she plotted to lure me into her home so she could bake me into some kind of stew or possibly touch my dick. Soon enough Becky was past the shut-in's house and Dave Jordan's house as well, Dave whose step-dad never spoke much after coming home from Vietnam and never could stand for any kind of noise in the yard.

I kept looking over my shoulder, but Becky was there, coming, coming after me, up the street and towards my house, and I was running, the sweat trickling down my back as I headed up the hill in front of my house and through the front door, where I was safe and could play Missile Command before I went out to see my friends because she was gone.

Except that she wasn't.

"Who's the girl sitting on the front lawn?" my dad asked, walking in. "She's cute." My dad wasn't living with us right then, but he was home to make dinner, because everything was going to be like it always was.

"Becky is on the front lawn?" I said.

"Becky? Sure. Should we invite her in?"

"No, no, what am I going to do?"

"Do, do about what?"

"Leaving the house!"

My dad paused. He knew something about leaving the house.

"Here's what you do," he said. "You put on your Lone Ranger mask and just leave, walk right by her, no eye contact, no looking back."

"Yeah?"

"Yeah. It'll work like a charm."

And so I did, never looking back and never really talking to her again.

"Hey, Becky," I say back at Thirsty's. "Can I get you a drink?"

"Are you sure?"

"Yeah, why?"

I know why. She knows why. We haven't talked in twenty-five years. Still, she looks good, decent. She has nice eyes, kind eyes. Plus, the fact is my wife Marsha is fucking our friend Tommie and I was the last to find out.

"I'll have a Yuengling," she says.

"Cool."

"Jamie," she yells, motioning Jamie over. "Another Yuengling."

"Two," I shout.

"Sure," he grunts.

Jamie walks over to the tap, nearly, but not quite out of earshot.

"Are you friends with him?" I ask Becky whispering, and looking-up, not wanting Jamie to hear us.

"Why?" she says leaning forward, then pulling back, placing her arms on her chest, crossing, then uncrossing them again.

"I don't know," I say. "He seems kind of weird with that bad bowl haircut and those fucked-up teeth. Well, and that shit back in high school."

Jamie had terrorized us when we were kids. He was bigger than we were. And mean. Smashing our ears on the bus with the palms of his hands; messing with our bikes by letting the air out of the tires, removing the seats, and disconnecting the brakes, if we left them unattended for even a second; endlessly pelting us with rocks, ice balls and crabapples; squeezing our nipples; or worse, our balls in the locker room after swim class, grabbing them hard, and gripping them tight, and then pausing, his smile malicious and hungry.

We knew enough to know his home life was fucked up, all poor and violent, but we didn't care, he was a fucking bully, and we all hated him, suppressing our anger and fear, because we couldn't fight him and there was no one to tell. No one's parents were ever around, and even if they had been, who was going to talk to Jamie's fat fucking father Joey? No one. No one's dad was that tough or scary.

And then he was gone, as if abducted by aliens, which we would have believed and enjoyed. But no, the rumor was that he had been sent to a home for juvenile delinquents. For what we didn't know, but did it matter? No. We were free, until we weren't. In high school the rumors started up again. Jamie was coming back. He had done his time. We all started to get tense and worked-up, afraid this hulking figure from our past would soon be haunting the corridors and locker rooms again.

If Jamie had been a bully before they sent him away, what would he be like now?

He wasn't a bully. He wasn't even tough. He was small, smaller than all of us, like he had stopped growing. And maybe he had. He was also soft. His shoulders perpetually bowed. Quiet, dressed in his Anderson-Little oxfords, he never spoke, never really looked up from the ground. He was scared of everything, you could smell it. Rumors were that he had been raped wherever it was they sent him, which seemed possible, because here he was, fucked up and different.

"I don't think any of that stuff people said about him was true," Becky says.

"No?" I reply.

"No. He had a rough time, but he's better now."

"Yeah? How do you know?" I ask, looking right at her.

"Can we talk about something else?"

"Sure. How about I walk you home?"

"Yeah, okay, why not."

We walk down Vestal Avenue towards Becky's house, past Robby's Liquor Store and the old post office. We walk into her house and we are both quiet, anticipating something that already seems likely to happen.

"Do you want a beer?" Becky asks me.

"Okay."

"So, your wife is banging Tommie," she says matter-of-factly.

"That's what I hear."

"Is that why you're here?"

"Can we talk about something else?"

"Yeah, okay. What?"

"You know what? Maybe we could just fuck."

"Okay, sure."

And so we fuck.

The next day I am at work and I am thinking about Becky and how it's even possible that I'm doing so all these years later. She told me that she's off work today, though it's not remotely clear to me that she actually does anything besides drink at Thirsty's. I walk over to Robby's during lunch, grab a six-pack of Yuengling and decide to surprise her.

For a moment I think about how I once met my wife for lunch, but I suppose I should finally admit to myself that she isn't just fucking Tommie any more, she lives with him now, and she's not coming home.

As I get to her house I see Jamie sitting on her porch. He's dragging a knife back and forth along the table in front of him. He looks up at me.

"Hey," I say. "What's up, man?"

"She's my fucking girlfriend," he says quietly, still dragging the knife, still looking at me.

What? Fuck. Seriously. How? I start to rub my leg with my hand. I don't respond. What can I say?

"You heard me," he shouts. "Becky is my fucking girlfriend, my *girlfriend*, my fucking *girlfriend*."

My heart starts to pound. "I-I-I didn't know," I stammer.

"My fucking girlfriend," he says, slamming the knife into the table, not moving, just sitting there and waiting for what happens next.

Becky opens the door. Jamie still doesn't move, but I wish he would. Becky's been crying. I don't feel bad, just furious, though why I do is hard to say.

"What the fuck," I say, ignoring Jamie, looking at Becky. "Jamie's your boyfriend?"

"Yeah," she says, her eyes puffy and tired-looking, like she's been crying all morning.

"What the fuck?"

64

She doesn't say anything. She's just staring off into space.

"Why didn't you say something?"

She's still just staring, reminding me so much of her mom when we were kids.

"What the fuck?!" I shout.

"You were making fun of him," she says, snapping back to attention, her voice choking. "And I wanted you, what was I supposed to say?"

"What are you, fucking five years old?"

Becky covers her face with her hands, still crying, her shoulders shaking.

"Seriously, why didn't you say something?"

Becky looks down at her feet. "Because it was you," she says, not looking back up.

"I don't know what that means," I say, though I do, no longer feeling enraged, just tired, "but you won't have to worry about it again ..."

I stop speaking as Jamie stands up and now by her side, puts his arm around Becky's shoulders. He doesn't look angry any more, just sad.

I turn to walk away, Becky's sobs ringing in my ears, but as I look out into the day, I realize that I have nowhere to go.

15

Sloe Gin Fizz is Pink

by Martha Rand

Sloe Gin Fizz is pink
Bombay Gin comes in blue
I'm sitting here at Emerald's
And all I can think of is –
you.

The little pause after "is" made it almost rhythmic. It's the most beautiful morning and the Emerald Bar will be closing soon. She's been up all night in the news room. Ohhh, the sacrifice of a nighttime job. She knows she has the best job she could possibly get in the best market in the country and so she's here on a Tuesday, drinking a Bloody Mary.

"Good night and good luck."

"Good night, good luck and be well."

"And so it goes."

These were words said at the end of shows by some of her favorite news anchors. She's been sitting at a bar where some of the biggest newsmen have sat before. Probably before the show, after the show, in between the shows, they'd been at that very same place on Columbus Avenue. She knows the guys with the liver spots they can't hide even under the thick pancake make-up. She doesn't wear that, she isn't the talent.

She's used to sacrifice. The only time she throws up in the morning, now, is when she's had too much to drink. No more sticking her fingers down her throat as part of her morning ritual. The calluses on her knuckles are gone, but she'll probably never have nice nails. Many possibilities are gone.

Although she dares to believe that many possibilities are still ahead.

There is the sudden sound of sirens. She looks out the front window and sees the fire engines racing downtown. The door opens with a rush of wind and a beautiful slice of sunlight splices the darkness at the doorway. The sirens are louder now.

"Do you know what's happening?" the man who entered shouts as he runs up to the bar. "Turn on the news."

Cartoons had been playing, because the newsies in the bar were off the clock.

The bartender points the remote toward the TV and clicks.

At first she can't tell what's happening. There's smoke. There's a tower. It's hard to see, but there's a plane sticking out of the building. It's a transfixing moment in which lifetimes are changing.

Her cell phone vibrates on the bar. She wasn't going to pick up, but then she thinks, Better.

The call's gone to voicemail before she can catch it.

Everything in her is shaking. "You think you've seen everything," she hears herself say, pulling a twenty out of her jacket pocket. The news studio is two blocks down.

16

Gullible

by Joanna Delooze

Jonas watched the woman nurse her second drink, idly pick at her manicure, glance at the clock. No one else was in the bar, everyone glued to the festival screens in the main hall, supposedly hushed and awed by the magnificence of yet another cinematic offering. It was obvious she couldn't care less.

He knew who she was. *Everyone* knew who she was. Time had been kind to her but it was catching up. When she'd slid between the double doors, displaced conversation from the movie followed her, then disappeared abruptly as the cushioned springs clicked softly shut.

"You speak English?" she asked.

"Ya," he said, with an accent quite a bit more pronounced than normal. It was that time of the year, play it up for the tourists.

"Thank goodness," she sighed, close to tears. He'd noticed her earlier, as she'd done the rounds in the lounge, on the arm of a producer many years her senior. Pneumatic, almost past her peak in the industry, along for the ride hoping it would spark renewed interest in her career. He'd seen it year after year. Different faces, same story.

"I need a drink. Anything as long as it has a bite. A big one."

"Rough night?"

"Wandering hands, bad breath. Then there's the performance later, if you know what I mean. I'm kind of tired of it all, you know?"

"Get a taxi and go home then. What's the worst that could happen?"

Half an hour. He'd be wondering where she was. As far as she was concerned, he could keep on wondering. The ulcer she thought she'd got rid of had screamed in protest when the alcohol hit it. A warm buzz crawled up from the soles of her shoes. Whatever he was giving her to drink, it was good. She was starting to not give a shit about any of it.

The external door opened, bringing a cool gust of air into the still room. The bartender looked up, just as she did, but she could tell by the look on his face that the man didn't register with him.

But he registered with her. The ulcer churned and spat venom.

Rupert Hayes. Movie producer. Bastard. Cheat. Fabulous in the sack. She looked around for something heavy to smash over his head. The last time she'd seen him (in person anyway) had been three years ago. He'd stood in her back garden, ankle deep in snow, his boxers flapping in the frigid wind. Begging her to let him back in.

"Gill? Who the hell is Gill?? You screamed her name while we were having sex, Roo! How stupid do you think I am?" She threw his trousers, shoes and wallet after him. Carefully aimed car keys nearly took out his left eye.

"People say stupid things all the time, Naomi. Honestly, it's nothing. Let me in, love, please. I'm dying out here!"

"*Goodbye*, Rupert. Don't call me."

Of course he did, repeatedly, leaving numerous frantic, lovelorn messages and one drunken, begging soliloquy the night before he married Gill.

"Just say the word, Naomi, just say it and I'll walk away right now, I won't marry her. Please honey, please, I don't love her. I still love you."

She blocked his calls, asked his secretary to stop pretending he wanted her to come in for castings, changed her number. She proceeded to run through an army of men trying to forget him.

Married or not, he wouldn't let her. He sent presents on her birthday, flowers on their anniversary.

And now here he was, standing in the doorway, his impeccable tuxedo rumpled, rain splattered and smeared on the shoulder with something that looked not unlike a splat of bird poop.

And he had a sleeping baby in his arms.

A baby?

She looked stunning as usual, but frustrated, indecisive, ready to run away. He watched her through the window for a minute, shielding the baby from the rain. Finally, God was smiling on him. No paying the bartender or a dodgy member of the theatre staff. No fumbling with his rusty primary school German. He looked at his watch. Just enough time. His film was screening in half an hour. Time enough to settle the baby, clean the sick off his suit, sort out his hair. No way he was going in there looking like this. Hiding his relieved smile, he arranged his face in a suitably downcast pose and pushed open the door.

"Do you speak English?" he asked, pretending he hadn't seen Naomi in the shadows at the end of the bar.

The bartender rolled his eyes. "Ya, what can I do for you?"

"I'm desperate, mate. My name is Rupert Hayes. I'm a producer from England. My au pair went sightseeing and never came back when she was supposed to. I can't raise her on the phone. *My film* is being screened in *half an hour*. I *have* to be out there. I have 500 euros cash for you if you can find me a babysitter for two and a half hours and another 500 for whoever you get to watch him for me. Someone reliable."

Right on cue she chimed in. "I'll do it. But I want to see the money *now*."

Damn. He'd have to stump up after all. At least he knew he could trust her not to leave the baby in a dumpster somewhere while she used the cash to get stoned. He turned, feigning surprise.

"Naomi? What are you doing here?"

"Saving your arse, apparently. Where's Gill? How come you're here with the au pair and not her?" She held out her palm, wiggling fingers for the cash. He dug it out reluctantly, juggling the baby on his shoulder.

"She was supposed to arrive yesterday. She phoned at breakfast and said she was going to Italy with her sister and I should expect divorce papers when I get back home. And I have no idea where the hell the bloody au pair is, I've been phoning her for hours."

"Give me the baby and the bag. Get cleaned up. We can talk after. What's his name?"

"Robbie. He just ate and it's his normal bedtime so he should stay asleep if it's quiet."

He stood to leave. She looked up at him, gears spinning behind her eyes. He'd seen that look enough times to know she'd sussed him.

"Roo, why'd she leave you?"

"Same problem. Can't keep bloody names straight, can I?"

She smirked, choking on her drink. He wondered if she was too drunk to manage the child, but knew it didn't matter. He really had no choice.

"More fool you. Whose name was it this time?" she laughed.

He walked to the door, not answering. Years in the business had taught him one thing: timing is everything. He paused, counted to three and turned back to her.

"Yours, love. It's always been yours."

Jonas watched her with the baby. She was good: attentive, entertaining and not at all concerned about the milky puke dripping down her creamy, exposed shoulders. It puddled along the rim of her navy satin ball gown. He imagined licking it off her warm skin, slowly drawing down the long silvery zip on the back of her dress.

Some guys had all the luck. He'd just lost 500 euros before he even had his fingers on it. And Rupert Hayes? Rupert Hayes was in the process of offloading his wife, had one of the sexiest women alive dandling his baby on her knee, was enjoying the accolades of a crowd that would most likely pick his film to win this weekend, *and*, if ten years behind this bar had taught Jonas anything about human nature, it was going to be Rupert Hayes slowly drawing down that long silvery zip later tonight.

As big a lie as they knew it to be, once that line left his lips, her face had said it all.

Gooey, lovestruck, forgiving.

No wonder the man was revered in the industry. Tonight had to be the snappiest production he'd ever pulled off. And he'd done it on the spur of the moment, with no assistants, hardly any budget, and only one actress on board.

Well, that's all you needed really, wasn't it?

One actress.

One *really gullible* actress.

17

Boxers

by Len Kuntz

After the funeral, my brother and I go to the nearest bar.

It's an Irish pub that plays authentic Gaelic folk songs. Framed pictures of castles and men in kilts hang lopsidedly from the walls. The air smells spiced and briny.

Over my brother's shoulders, there's a boxing match on television. A black guy is beating the shit out of a smaller Hispanic fighter, but the ref doesn't seem to notice.

"I'm glad that's over," my brother says, and for a second I'm not sure if he means the funeral or our father's life.

"You did a nice job," I say, because I know he's expecting it, though he does tuck in his chin, blushing, while muttering, "Thanks."

My brother looks like a younger, thinner version of our Dad – movie star handsome. He gave the eulogy. No other option had been discussed. My brother's performance was pitch-perfect, veering off surprisingly at one point when his voice caught the kind of cadence Southern preachers affect, thumping alliteration and repetition, building his speech up to a magnificent crescendo. The crowd – dour until then – loved it and even applauded.

On TV a new round is starting. The Hispanic guy's got his elbows tucked against his ribs. He takes two sharp jabs that snap his head back. His right eye is purple and swollen to the size of a small squid. I wonder why the ref doesn't stop the fight or why the Hispanic guy's trainer doesn't throw out the white towel.

During the eulogy my brother listed all of the favorable characteristics he thought our father possessed. My brother told poignant stories about sacrifices made during our childhood – often holding several jobs simultaneously, putting in eighty-hour work weeks. But my brother never mentioned the beatings Dad gave our mother. He never mentioned how we watched them happening, unable to stop them, or about the time we hid out with Mom at Aunt Judy's until the raging bear drove right up on Aunt Judy's lawn, blaring the horn until we walked out the door, palms clutched like kidnapped victims being released.

My brother twirls his finger in the air at the waitress and says, "'Nother round," without asking me.

On TV, the Hispanic takes a brutal uppercut to the chin. They show it over and over in slow motion, how he's lifted a few inches off the mat, blood and sweat wicking the air like a grotesque sneeze, the fighter then landing and crumpling instantly.

My brother is flying out tonight. The funeral's already caused him to miss part of an important conference. I've been with him all three times he's phoned his wife, and at the close of each call he told her he loved her, never altering the inflection of his voice because of my presence.

My own wife is back at the hotel. She doesn't know the dark things about Dad, and I realize now that I'll never tell her. Instead, I'll hold my tongue, flatten my hands, and put them to good use. I've never been like my father, not at all, and I never want to be.

18

Holiday

by S.H. Gall

My reedy frame was cloaked in a heavy down parka that night at the Holiday. It was uncomfortably warm in the room to begin with, perhaps with the collective yearning of many souls, but the parka had one useful quality. It was handy for casually brushing up against bodies. And one body in particular.

There were precious few men to my liking that night, which was typical. I was very young, so young I was swilling gin & tonics in the pit of winter. I had a boyfriend. We had sex quite often, yet I still craved more on the side. My guy was Croatian. I sought an Italian.

There were a few interactions with random strangers who sat on the next stool. Small talk mostly, followed by abrupt turn-downs. All it took was a rueful smile and a turn of the head. Meaningless, because they weren't my type. Mine was a shallow world. There was a particular guy I liked who usually could be found on any given night, waiting to get fucked in the back of his conversion van. He was the oldest of my conquests, but insatiable despite his age. Not tonight, though. I was about to throw in the towel when I saw him.

Brown eyes, check. Noble nose, check. Other details fell by the wayside. The bathroom was in the basement, and as I meandered down to it, I made a point of letting my heavy coat brush the man's back as I passed. After three such forays to the filthy john, he turned his head, curious as to why my coat kept making contact with his back. With some hesitancy he got up, and led me to the door.

He could scarcely believe I'd chosen him, but the quilted brush – more like a light smack – of the parka left him no choice but to accept. He lived just a few blocks away. I don't recall the walk, but my recollection of our stripping down once in his living room is impeccable. He was short, and hairy, and his mouth tasted of garlic and Campari. Well-hung. Snow white tan. Unmistakably Italian.

I didn't get his digits. Two weeks later, I was standing outside his building, throwing snowballs at his window to get his attention. Somewhat incredulously, he accepted my offer for another encounter. And then there were others.

I stayed with my boyfriend, had affairs with many men, mostly married. But the Italian from the Holiday refused to leave my head. The Croatian finally left town, not willing to support my bad habits, not willing to continue couples therapy, eager to soak in his beloved California sun. I went further down the rabbit hole, finally discovering bona fide insanity. An antidepressant I was taking caused a psychotic break, and I ended up in the hospital on a Valium drip.

I've been with the Italian for over a decade now ... and officially, as a couple, for four years and counting. The Holiday is closed now, the building demolished. But as I sit on the bus and pass the site, I can see it clear as day. It was a beginning.

Sobriety Group

by Gloria Garfunkel

The Sobriety Group met at four every Wednesday night, just in time for the seven members to get a good table at Patrick's bar to drink beer by six.

"Beer's not really even alcohol," laughed one and then all.

This had been going on for nine months, since they were all sentenced for driving under the influence, with daily AA meetings and a weekly therapy group.

At the group meetings, they claimed remorse over all their losses: relationships, family, finances, with a young female therapist who clearly knew nothing about alcoholics and was easy to fool. They drew straws who would cry and do the blubbering that week. They called themselves screw-ups, failures, fuck-ups, assholes and she gently empathized and soothed.

Only three more months of this charade and Larry, driving home drunk from the bar, hit and killed a nine-year-old girl on a bike.

Last Call at the Do Drop Inn

by Arthur Carey

Charlie Jointer swept through the doors of the Do Drop Inn just in time to hear Tiny the bartender's final warning: "Five minutes until Cinderella time!" Lights strung haphazardly around the mirror behind the bar flickered on and off in case anyone hadn't paid attention.

Charlie slid onto a worn vinyl seat as the few remaining customers started to leave. He began drawing vigorous circles in the air to get Tiny's attention. A short, round-shouldered man with graying hair and steel-rimmed glasses, Charlie was used to being overlooked on bar stools. Once seated, he vanished like a sapling among redwood trees.

As he served the last holdouts, Tiny caught the signal and nodded. He poured a shot of Jack Daniel's for Emilio Garcia, who downed the drink quickly. Garcia tossed two singles on the bar and walked out with short, careful steps, leaning on a scarred wooden cane. The LaRues, Rose and Gus, debated in low voices whether to order a final drink. Rose won. They pushed back from the bar. "G'night, Tiny," mumbled Gus.

"Am I gonna get a beer here or do I die of thirst?" asked Charlie, his voice ringing in the empty saloon.

"Coming up," said Tiny. "Think I'll join you before cleaning up." He locked the door to latecomers and drew a schooner of beer for Charlie and one for himself. He walked around the bar and sat down next to the smaller man.

Relaxing, the bartender's broad shoulders sagged as if a coat hanger supporting them had been removed.

"Tough night?" asked Charlie.

"Nah … just long. I worked a double shift. The morning guy called in sick and the owner couldn't fill in. I don't usually see you this time of night."

Charlie stifled a yawn. "I caught a late movie, that dumb comedy about the guys who go to Vegas and wind up the next morning hung over with no idea what happened the night before. Then I stopped at the coffee shop for a piece of pie." He took a swallow of beer. "Maybe I should give that a try, you know, going to Vegas. I wouldn't need to burn any vacation time. It's all vacation time from now on."

"How long until the plant closes?" asked Tiny.

"The last car rolls out in two days. We got written notices this morning," said Charlie. "Then it's all over for me after twenty-six years. Assembly … finishing … quality control … I done it all."

"No chance the company will extend the closing? They got all the bad PR they can handle now with those mechanical problems."

Charlie shook his head. "The union was lucky to get the severance we asked for. Even then some of the guys out on disability may wind up screwed. The politicians got their headlines, blew a little smoke up our skirts and moved on." He looked in the mirror and grimaced. A worn, lined face stared back at him through large aviator-style glasses, long out of fashion. I'm like my truck, he thought bitterly … old, used up and ready for the scrap heap.

"Once the layoffs start, we'll take a hit, too," said Tiny. "Bad times hurt the bar business. People stay home and drink."

"At least you'll still have a job," Charlie grunted. "Where do I go at fifty-two with only a high school diploma and no experience except on an auto line? Nowhere, that's where. Pushing burgers and fries at McDonald's? I couldn't even operate the cash register and I don't know Spanish." He looked at Tiny. "You're still young and you been to college. What are you, twenty-three … twenty-four …?"

"I'm twenty-seven, Charlie. My best days are behind me. Just ask my girlfriend."

Charlie laughed but not at the joke. "Twenty-seven? Give me a break! You've got time to ride out this lousy economy. What about me? I'm still a decade or so away from Social Security and my working life is over – at least the good-paying part of it."

Tiny shrugged. "We don't always get what we want. I didn't go to college to wind up behind a bar five nights a week. I got a football scholarship to State. Blew out my left knee during practice my sophomore year. So I decided to get a master's degree in sports communications – better job opportunities I thought – and racked up a debt of 14,000 bucks along the way."

Charlie whistled.

Tiny shrugged. "Being young and having a college degree isn't a ticket to the good life any more. I've still got $4,000 to pay off on that loan. I could paper the restroom with the resumés I've sent out. There's nothing out there now, amigo ... nada."

Charlie nodded. "After Toyota started up here in '84, I thought I had it made – high-paying union job with benefits! I had lucked out and got hired by one of those Jap companies that provide jobs for life. Then they pulled the plug."

He took a sip of beer. "The newspapers said Toyota was looking all over the country for a place to locate. Everybody thought the plant would wind up in the South where labor was cheap. The San Francisco Bay Area? Nobody thought that's where it was supposed to go. But we wound up with the prize."

His mouth tightened. "Some prize. What's happened to this country, Tiny? Nothing seems to work any more. The jobs have vanished overseas. You read the paper and Iraq and Afghanistan never seem to go away regardless of who's in the White House. The debt ceiling? Those assholes in Washington can't agree on what to have for lunch. The banks get bailed out but lots of hard-working people are seeing their homes and life savings go down the toilet." He drained his glass.

Tiny rose and walked behind the bar. He drew two small beers and returned.

"Where were we?" asked Charlie.

"You were whining about how your life has turned to crap and you're not even out of a job yet," said Tiny.

Charlie straightened up. "Wait ... I wasn't ..."

"Sure, you were. And I was about to gripe about how I never got to star on Monday night football – or be a TV commentator, sucking up to the guys who did."

"Okay, okay, I hear you," Charlie grumbled. "I'll cancel the pity parade."

Tiny raised his glass in a toast that wasn't really a toast. "Feel any better now?"

He got an exasperated look in return. "No. Was I supposed to?"

Tiny shrugged. "Sometimes you ride the wave and sometimes the wave rides you."

"So you're a surfer and philosopher as well as a bartender," Charlie said. He drained his glass and reached for his wallet.

"On the house," said Tiny. "Don't tell the boss."

"No charge for the nickel and dime therapy?"

"No, that's free, too."

Tiny eased off the bar stool and walked to the door. He pulled out a ring of keys on a chain, selected one, and unlocked the door.

Charlie zipped up his jacket. "Thanks ... I think."

He stepped out into the chill night air. Rain had fallen and muddy puddles dimpled the dirt parking lot. Charlie picked his way to a ten-year-old Toyota pickup. The faded red paint gleamed dully in the light from the bar. As he fumbled for keys, the 'Welcome' sign over the entrance winked out.

Waiting with Merle

by Ramon Collins

When Mike entered the Back 40 Lounge he was greeted by the subtle aroma of secondhand smoke and Lysol. He stopped, squinted against the murk and rubbed his eyes – Jolene perched on a stool near the end of the bar. Mike straddled a stool halfway down.

Jolene shot a sidelong glance. "So how ya been?"

"Gets kinda lonely. Grubby motel room, TV movies and peanut butter sandwiches." Mike stared down his beer.

She snubbed out a cigarette. "If I remember correct, you're the one that said you wanted to split the sheet – it's damn-well split."

"I was half-hammered." He fidgeted on the bar stool. "Dammit, a man can change. If he gets a chance, that is."

"I felt lucky when you changed your shorts."

Smitty came around the bar, b-e-l-c-hed, punched some buttons on the jukebox and Merle Haggard sang about love. Mike slid one stool closer to her; his brow furrowed as he studied a cracked tile on the floor.

"Tell me, Jo – do I ever cross your mind?"

"For chrissake, you've only been gone two nights."

Mike watched a piece of foam slide down the side of his glass as Willie Nelson sang about a good-hearted woman, in love with a good-timin' man.

First Time

by Andrew J. Stone

It began as a mistake.

The Greedy Pig, a smalltime bar in Vancouver. I was nineteen and American. And besides the strange name, two things hooked me: Joe Strummer's voice bleeding from the speakers and the plasma TV playing the Canucks game. And yeah, outside, sheets of rain were falling fast and hard.

Inside the bar the rain turned to sweat. I found an open seat, sat down and the bartender asked what'd it be. It would be rum on the rocks.

He served me quick. And then he served me a second one even quicker. The Canucks were down by three to those goddamned Blackhawks, and the bartender was telling me how he didn't give much of a damn about the Canucks this season.

"The Olympics are where it is at," he said. "Alex Pietrangelo, a Canadian-born defenseman playing for the St. Louis Blues, is where it is at."

"Right," I said.

I thought I saw seven empty glasses on the bar in front of me. And I pressed the eighth to my lips. That might have been why I bought drinks for the girl sitting next to me. Or it might have been because she was inching her hand up my thigh. Or was she doing that because I was buying her booze? I don't know. But I bought her a round and ordered myself another rum on the rocks.

The girl's name is Tabatha. She's not American or Canadian.

"I'm English," she said.

"You disguise your accent pretty well. It's disappointing."

"Yeah?"

"Yeah."

"My accent doesn't bother anyone else. Hey, Danny," she said, and the bartender approached us. "My accent bother you?"

"No."

She looked smug, too smug for my liking. I said, "Why so smug?"

"My accent doesn't bother Danny." She winked.

"What are you doing out here in Vancouver?" I said.

"Visiting my fiancé. It was a surprise. And I walked in on him fucking some bitch. He'll never fuck again."

Never fall on her bad side, I thought.

"How about you. Why are you here?"

I ordered another round. I let that be my answer.

It got late. The drinks kept coming. Then they stopped coming. I wanted to know why.

"Danny must've cut us off," Tabatha said. "Hey Danny, go fuck yourself."

"Hey Stevie, handle them?" Danny laughed.

The bouncer did what he was told.

In the rain, Tabatha took my hand. "Where are you staying?" she asked.

I said something and she led the way. We eventually made it to the hotel. I undressed. I blacked out.

In the morning, Tabatha was gone. I never saw her again, but I asked some people, the right kind of people, some questions, and they gave me some answers. And before I left Vancouver I learned a few things about Tabatha. She was not English. She never had a fiancé. She had everything I brought to Vancouver except for a single pair of clothes. She was beautiful.

23

Coffin Showroom

by Claudia Bierschenk

"You must be Mister Jones."

Her river pebble hand delicate in mine. Will she spot the worn seam of my right jacket sleeve?

My dry throat croaks, "Hello".

"Please, Mister Jones, do come in."

A shoe shelf stacked with felt slippers. I hesitate.

"Oh, I hope you don't mind taking off your shoes. We feel that the sound of heels disturbs the atmosphere," she says. Her dark, soft voice matches the slight rustle of her dress. She smiles.

I would simply ask her where the nearest bar is, later. It's a perfectly normal thing to ask.

Faint music echoes through the showroom. The air conditioning purrs. Sweat trickles down the small of my back. Leave the jacket on. Ice. Order something with ice. In a tall glass.

They are arranged in an elevated circle. She talks about the advantages of this one and the price of that one, comments on the customized interiors, touches them. My lips manage a dry, "Uh-huh." Bubbles. The first sip. Cider. A summer drink.

There is a nice one, in the corner: I flap over to the sleek metal finish. The smell of leather pulls me in. She speaks to my shoulder. "Oh, this is a deluxe model. Only made to order." The wood, dark and machined, like a bar counter. Funny idea: a barroom for the dead. What will you have? Same as yourself.

She clears her throat.

"I am sorry," I say, "What did you say?"

"Delivery time, Mister Jones. We must allow for delivery time."

"Two weeks." My fingers gripping the side of the coffin.

She raises plucked eyebrows.

"I will see what I can do," she says, smoothing down the dress over her hips. Something buzzes in her pocket. "Please excuse me for a moment," she says, and shuffles away fondling the dress pocket for her mobile phone.

I shuck off the slippers, pull over a chair and, one, two, lower myself into the casket. The leather is cool and smooth. I sigh and close my eyes.

24

One Night at Harry's

by Alun Williams

I never knew anyone could smoke so many cigarettes and still have the ability to play piano like he did. Maybe cancer doesn't affect the hands. I don't know if that's correct 'cause I'm not a doctor, but his fingers, stained desert yellow from years of nicotine abuse never lost their magic. By the time he reached thirty he was thin, gaunt and looking twenty years older. I can honestly say I never saw him eat anything more than ice in a whisky sour on the rocks. It was his staple diet along with sixty Camels a day.

Johnson Browne never usually talked much to customers; I don't think he had the energy after his shows, but that last Christmas Eve, when the winter snows had almost closed the city down, he sat down at his piano at Harry's Bar and played the show of his life to me, Walter the barkeep, and an old black drunk called Smitty.

None of us had anyplace else to go or anyplace else we'd want to be. When Christmas comes, people like us tend to stick together. Harry's Bar is our comfort church and we had more than a hundred reasons to be there and not one to stay at home.

Johnson didn't have to play that evening, not to an almost deserted bar. But he lit one cigarette, took his jacket off and played. Piano keys will never be played like that again. I think he must have smoked a hundred cigarettes that night and drank at least fifteen whisky sours. He played anything and everything from jazz and blues to ragtime and Mozart.

The last song he played was 'Silent Night'. Johnson looked up and saw the snow falling out the window and played it like I'd never heard it played before, then at the end of his piece he joined us for one last drink. I told him it was the greatest piece of piano playing I'd ever heard. He shrugged his shoulders, wiped his sweaty brow and lit another cigarette. He said one word, "Thanks," put his coat on, and shuffled out into a Chicago winter.

I guess no one knew what really happened that night, but a mailman found his body early next morning, frozen stiff. He had a smile on his face and a half smoked Camel between his lips.

No one plays piano at Harry's Bar anymore.

25

Union Jack

by Paul Combs

I'm sitting at the bar minding my own damn business when a 300 pound leprechaun stumbles over his elf shoes and nearly knocks me off my stool. Green beer sloshes out of my mug and onto the floor. St. Patrick's Day in an Irish bar comes with hazards, and Lucky here is the least of them. I look at his green elf hat and glass eye with the shamrock for a pupil and remember arresting him about a year ago.

Even calling The Blarney Stone an Irish bar seems a stretch. The décor is more what you would find in a kitschy Italian restaurant, the walls covered with photographs of Italian celebrities from Sinatra to the Pope. The only evidence of an Emerald Isle connection is a large Irish flag above the stage and a sign that reads: 'Dogs and Englishmen Not Allowed'.

Ethnicity aside, it's a typical college hangout with one notable exception: no dance floor. That's only noticeable because of the number of girls trying to dance beside the tables. Each time a girl's hips move more than they would when walking, a bouncer rushes over and stops them.

"Well good evening, my boy," a voice says coldly from the other side of the bar. "Another beer?"

I look over and see James Donovan: bar owner, father of my new girlfriend Kathleen, mobster.

"Hello, sir. Sure."

He leans down to grab a mug and catches a glimpse of the tattoo peeking beneath the edge of my sleeve.

"What the fuck is that?" he snarls.

I push the sleeve further up my bicep to reveal a Union Jack inside the outline of a heart.

"It's a tattoo."

"Don't be a wise-ass, boy," Donovan says. "You see that sign over there?" He points to the 'Dogs and Englishmen Not Allowed' sign.

"I saw it, but I'm a Texan. It's my mom who's English. From Manchester."

"Figures. And what about your dad? He a bloody Brit too?"

"German. And a Federal Prosecutor."

Donovan's face flushes crimson, but before he can speak someone is behind me, tapping me on the shoulder.

"Your table's ready, sir."

I turn to see a waitress, maybe eighteen years old with dyed-green hair, holding a tray of drinks. She gives me a quick smile.

"Right this way. There's an empty table over here."

I slide off the stool, but Donovan stops me.

"Is that true about your dad?" he asks. I knew that would get him.

"No," I lie. "He's actually a mechanic, but after you disrespected my mom ..."

Donovan smiles, then nods.

The waitress seats me at a small table near the stage and puts down a shot. She turns to leave but I put a hand on her arm.

"Why is there no dancing allowed?"

"Zoning ordinance," she says. "We're too close to the First Baptist Church."

Before I can ask what the hell this means there's a deafening crash a few tables away. Then shouting and fists flying and the smack of bones and muscle. A wild-eyed, solid man wades into the scrum, cracking guys' heads, knees, backs, shoulders with a sawed-off pool cue as he goes. It's Eddie Donovan, Kathleen's brother. I recognize him from the mug shot the Feds gave me.

One beefy guy punches a bystander in the face, who crumples in a heap. Eddie steps from his blind side, dislocates his knee with the cue, and cracks the guy on top of the head as he falls. His blood spurts across Eddie's face, but Eddie just keeps swinging his pool cue. His father sprints to his side faster than I expect for a man of his bulk.

"Hey, you little shit," he says, glaring down at the guy, "stop bleeding on my floor." His voice is cold, flat, devoid of emotion.

"I've got him, Pop," Eddie says, grabbing the man by the collar.

Old man Donovan claps a meaty hand on his son's shoulder.

"We pay people for that kind of scut work, son," he says, and steers Eddie back to the bar. Both men grin at me, shove through the gawking crowd and past my table; Eddie slaps the bloody pool cue into his open palm.

The show now over, I throw back the shot of whiskey the waitress left.

Suddenly the crazy-eyed brother is back, sitting at my table, still slapping the pool cue into his palm. His smile has vanished, his mouth now a tight slit, and blood still drips from his face; for a second I think I'll have to shoot him, which will totally fuck my cover. Before I can reach for the gun in my boot Kathleen appears behind her brother. She grabs one of his ears and jerks down hard, yanking him out of the chair and onto his knees.

"Jesus!" he screams. "Let me go, you crazy bitch!"

"I told you not to pull any of your crazy macho shit!" she screams back. She looks over at her father, who is grinning broadly. "I told both of you."

She throws a vicious knee into her brother's spine and he pitches face-first onto the floor.

"Let's go," she says. "There's an English pub down the street with a more agreeable clientele."

We walk past her father behind the bar.

"Enjoy your evening lad," he says. "My daughter won't always be around to protect you."

As we stride across the parking lot I grab her hand; it feels hot. I glance at her face; she is flushed and beaming. At that moment I realize my new angel could be the most dangerous Donovan of all. Maybe I'll use my handcuffs on her later.

26

Hollywood Cemetery

by Christine Cook

He found her at a bar while he drank a glass of whiskey. She looked at him sideways. He looked over and away a few times before she walked over to him.

"Why are you here so early?" she asked, setting her glass of cheap white wine down on the bar.

"I don't know," he said. "Why are you here?"

"I asked you first," she said. He looked her up and down, deciding she was at least 5 years younger than his 31.

"I'm attempting to get mildly drunk before attending my grandfather's funeral," he said.

"Only mildly?"

"Well yes," he replied, trying to stop his eyelids, heavy with sleep, from drooping. "I can't fall over at my grandfather's funeral. Who the fuck does that?"

"You could do that," she said, sitting down and tucking her legs under the stool. "Why are you so afraid of going to his funeral anyway? He's already dead."

He turned to her. Was she entirely fucked up or onto something? Her eyes were large, outlined in dark kohl, her deep brown eyes held his gaze and after an uncomfortable moment, he looked down and studied the wooden floor.

"I missed the last grandfather's funeral," he said.

"So now you have no grandfathers?"

"Everyone's pissed at me. Like it's my fault there's no grandfathers left."

"Well, where have you been?" she asked.

Josh had been gone for a long time, traversing the globe: getting drunk in Berlin, smoking hash in Amsterdam, fighting commuters in Tokyo.

"On tour, in a band. I'm the drummer in a folk band," he said, a twinge of disgust on his lips.

"So you're in a folk band, but you don't like their music?"

"Too many fucking harmonies."

"So not Bob Dylan folk?"

He shook his head.

"What's the name of the band?"

They were slightly more than famous. "Nothing you'd know," he said.

She unfolded her legs under the stool; pushed her shoulders back, crossed her arms against her body. "So why are you the drummer? Are you moody? Can you not be trusted with a microphone?"

"Ha-fucking-ha," he rolled his eyes at her, though maybe that *was* part of it. "I don't know why I'm the drummer, just how it worked I guess."

He took a swig of whiskey and clanked it back down on the bar.

He stared at the empty glass. "Maybe I'm moody."

"*I'm* moody," she said.

"I think I already knew that."

"So you like to be offensive too? What are you going to say to your mother at your grandfather's funeral?"

He looked at her. Not even a trace of anger graced her face. "Are you in love?"

"Who would I love?" she asked.

"A boy. A man. A woman," he said. "I don't know who you would love."

"I've been in love once or twice," she said. "Maybe a few more if I'm feeling sentimental."

He noted her short black dress, red nails, lips colored pink. And grinned.

"Do you want to come with me? You're already wearing black. I'll tell them you're my girlfriend."

She shrugged. "I've done worse."

"Great," he said.

She stared at her wine glass, moving her finger around the rim, while he studied his fingernails, bitten to the quick.

"What's your name anyway?"

"Alison. Allie. You?"

"Joshua. Well, Josh."

They didn't shake hands, it didn't seem right.

"So why are you in a bar at 11am?" he asked.

"Trying to get mildly drunk before the day starts," she replied, taking a large gulp from her wine glass.

The bright summer sun mocked the funeral procession as it moved slowly down the street. His feet felt large and clumsy as he walked behind the tiny figure of his grandmother.

They walked on cobblestone, into the cemetery, and Josh tried to remember the last time he had moved in a straight line or been quiet for this long. Light cast shadows across the manicured lawn and painted pictures on rows of headstones. The summer humidity choked him, the air too heavy to inhale; beads of sweat dripped down the back of his neck.

"Your hair has gotten too long," his mother had said when he arrived at the church. Now she stood behind him and he thought only of her watching his ponytail. Josh's shoes, polished and tight around the toes, usually banished to the bottom of his suitcase, sank into the grass, damp from watering. Family members stood surrounding the hole in the ground. Aunt Marion, hair pulled into a listing beehive; cousin James, face carved out from the effects of heroin. Despite the sun, the scene was cold and grey.

Allie took his hand and he looked down at her, confused. She smiled, her mouth crooked, her dark hair tucked behind her ears, and Josh watched a drop of sweat roll from her neck to the shoulder of her dress. She pulled a bottle of Jack Daniels from her purse.

She stood on the tips of her toes to reach his ear. "I took it from the bar," she whispered. "I thought you might need it."

He raised his eyebrows and looked around as she twisted off the cap and took a swig. If anyone noticed, they weren't concerned. Allie passed it to him and head back, he drank from the bottle until his throat stung.

As the mahogany casket began its descent into the ground, his grandmother broke the silence with a sad, small cry. She shuffled forward, a red rose cradled in her palm, and stood at the edge of the hole. Turning toward Josh, she looked him up and down, met his eyes and scowled before turning away and throwing the rose on the receding coffin. Josh squeezed Allie's fingers with one hand and tightened his grip on the bottle with the other.

27

Happy Anniversary

by Joyce Juzwik

I slid my right hand into the pocket of my jeans and felt the gun. It was cold and threatening. I will be its guide, and once the target is down, it will bring me final peace.

ROB
AND
RITA'S
PLACE

My destination. My destiny. Up in lights. A tired, weather-worn sign. Blue and green neon.

Talk is that it's a cozy neighborhood tavern. It's a dump. I knew it would be.

Death paid a visit here thirty years ago, and it stands beside me tonight. Ready and waiting.

Entering this pathetic excuse for a watering hole revealed fixtures and furniture akin to a 1950's sitcom set. Time had stopped here on that fateful night. Balloons bobbed on the tables and party hats were strewn across the bar. But I knew of nothing worth celebrating.

Over and over, my mother had told me the story of that horrific night.

I was almost a year old and asleep in the back seat of the 1983 Toyota Corolla station wagon my Mom and Dad had stolen from the auto dealer two weeks, and two counties, ago. Their salesman learned the hard way he should have accompanied them on their test drive. Back then, there was trust, and it was also no big deal to let a child sleep while Mom and Dad ran into the market for milk, or into a business to steal the take. That was how my parents made their living. You point a gun, Mom said, clerks hand over the cash, you drive away, and hit the next town. No problem. But that night, it all went wrong.

They had walked into a dive called Rob and Rita's in Fairvale, and Dad showed his gun and ordered the few customers to stand together on one side of the room while Mom told the woman behind the bar to hand over the cash. The wife, Rita, was working the bar while her husband, Rob, worked the kitchen. My father saw Rita reach under the bar and, believing Mom was in danger, shot Rita dead. Rob retrieved the gun they kept in the storeroom at the back of the kitchen and came out shooting. Hit my dad right between the eyes. There was nothing my mother could do for him, so she ran to the car and we made our getaway. She told me she couldn't allow herself to be captured since there was no one else to care for me.

Before she died, my mother made me promise to kill the man who had taken the life of my father. That woman, that Rita, she said, got what she deserved.

A man with a full head of curly white hair got up from his bar stool to greet me. I released my grip on the 9mm in my pocket and shook his hand. The only other customer was an elderly gray-haired woman sitting at a table next to the entry to the kitchen. Inspecting her basket of fries, her trembling hands brought a half glass of beer to her lips. Their presence was of no concern to me since once I accomplished my goal, I planned to remove myself from the equation. No punishment for me. Not any more.

"Come on in, son," he said. "This isn't a private party. This is Betsy Miller and you can call me Salty. I'll get you a beer. Rob's in the back getting some of the good stuff so we can drink a toast. Betts and I are the only ones left from the night when ... well, we make sure we come every year on his anniversary out of respect. Have a seat."

Betsy never looked up to acknowledge me. When Salty introduced us, she began taking the fries, one at a time, from the basket and placing them in a stack on the table. She uttered a small squeal of delight when her search revealed a packet of ketchup. If I'd had enough bullets, I'd have put them all down.

"You're not from here, are you?" Salty asked. "You look familiar though. Before Rob comes back, let me explain. See, thirty years ago tonight, we were celebrating Rob and Rita's first anniversary. There was more of us then, including my wife Sarah, and Bett's husband Ralphie. They've all passed though, so it's just us now.

"Rob went to get the champagne when this couple came in waving guns and asking for money. Rita reached down to get the cash and the woman shot her right in the face. I couldn't believe it. Everybody knew they never had any weapons. The man, who I had seen in here a couple of times before, asked his woman why she did that since the wife was just getting the box."

Everyone knew what? The woman shot who? I drank my beer in one gulp and slid the glass on the bar toward Salty.

"Haven't seen anybody do that since I was your age, young fella. Let me refill that for you. Anyhow, so Rob came running in from the kitchen and went over to check on Rita, who was lying face down on the floor behind the bar. When he turned her over and saw the damage the bullet had done to her head, he knew she was dead.

"The man was angry, waving his gun in the air as he approached his woman, and yelled at her that nobody was supposed to get hurt and asking her how she could be so stupid. He tried to grab her gun and they were struggling and it went off and the man fell down. She had shot her own man. She dropped her gun, pushed her way behind the bar, grabbed the tin box and ran out the door. We heard a car start up, but by the time we got outside, the woman was gone.

"Rob buried Rita a couple of days later. Found out when the doctor gave her the once over that she was a couple months' pregnant. She had told Rob she had a surprise for him at their anniversary party. I guess that was it."

I couldn't believe what I was hearing. This couldn't be true. It's the town's self-serving version of the massacre of my family. I wrapped my hand around the Glock in my pocket again. I hoped I had at least one extra bullet for this decrepit old liar.

"Terrible thing. If they had needed money, Rob would have given them some. Supper too, and a place to sleep in the back, if they needed it. The police identified both of them through their fingerprints on the guns, but they never did track the woman down."

Fingerprints? They probably figured out which gun killed Rita and which gun killed my father. Now, I knew too. My mother's gun killed them both. Dizziness washed over me and I grabbed the bar with both hands so as not to fall off the stool. My life thus far had been built on a foundation of lies.

"Finally. Done." Rob Tranley came out from the kitchen carrying a tray of sandwiches and placed it on the bar. He went back to the kitchen and brought out three chilled mugs and an open bottle of champagne.

"I see we have a new friend to help us celebrate. Welcome. Here, son, you can have my cold glass. I'll grab one from the shelf. Wait a sec. Do I know you? You've been here before, haven't you? Salty, Betts, doesn't he look familiar?"

"He does at that," Salty said. "Let your beer sit, son. You're looking a bit green around the gills. Betsy, come get a sandwich. Any roast beef, Rob?"

"On the bottom, Salty. Move the ham and cheese ones to the side." Rob filled each mug with champagne.

Betsy took a ham and cheese sandwich back to her table and started pulling it apart, layer by layer.

My stomach twisted into a knot. I'd seen photos. I was the mirror image of my father.

"Today's my anniver ... would be my anniversary – my wife passed away, but I still celebrate the day. Join us, please."

The man I had come here to kill set a plate with a sandwich on it and a mug of champagne on the bar in front of me. Rob and Salty picked up their mugs and turned to face me. Betsy was talking to the ketchup packet she had retrieved.

"To Rita," Rob said quietly. "Happy Anniversary."

"A good woman," Salty said. "Ditto."

I raised my glass. "Yes," I said. "Ditto."

28

Lefty, Daisy, and the Clueless Man

by Matt McGee

Lefty had been watching Daisy across the pub, but she'd been too busy to notice. Her eyes would slip every few seconds, checking to see if the guy in the pale blue dress shirt holding half a Stella and laughing with his co-worker bro's was noticing her. She tried not to be obvious, but Lefty watched her eyes betray her again and again. Seeing the empty stool beside her, he walked over. She didn't acknowledge him, but she knew he was there.

"Hi, I'm Lefty."

She couldn't help but give him the look.

"Yeah, Lefty," he answered. "And this is where you say you are ..."

"Not at all interested."

"Oh, I know you're not. I didn't sit down to get your number or start a mad-texting affair. I saw you," he pointed across the room, "from over there. I wanna help."

"Help?"

"Yeah. With the guy in the shirt. Mr. Big Hair."

She spoke at Lefty's widening forehead. "Don't let your jealousy shine through."

"Co-worker?"

"What?"

"He's your co-worker. You like him, you think he likes you but he's too shy or scared to make a move outside his little Guy Sanctuary. Maybe he's afraid of a sexual harassment suit. So he goes on talking sports, glad-handing the boys, wanting to talk to you but doesn't."

"And this is your business because ..."

"Don't look a gift-horse in the mouth, miss ..."

"Daisy."

"Seriously?"

"It's what Mom & Dad gave me. Lefty."

"Looks to me like they gave you a whole lot more, but that's not important. What's important is that smiling at a total stranger hitting on you in a pub, flipping your hair and looking at him will help you get Mr. Hair talking to you."

"What?"

"Just do it," he smiled.

"Screw you."

"No, see that's all wrong. DON'T do that. Smile at me. C'mon. A little. Pretend I'm gassy. That's it. Now a little more. OK stop, you don't wanna look like a Kardashian."

"Why am I doing this?" she said through her teeth.

"Because it's going to work. Now laugh. As if I've said something that's actually funny."

"What?"

Lefty smiled and said: "Just laugh ya big jerk!"

She let out a quick sarcastic burst. "OK that sucked," said Lucky. "Not like that, like this!" He burst into what appeared to be a sincere laugh as if she'd said something genuinely hilarious. She couldn't help herself and laughed at him.

"OK," she said through a gasp of air, "what am I doing ...?"

Lefty looked in the mirror behind the bartender; they'd caught dress-shirt guy's attention. "Yes! OK, now I'm gonna touch your forearm and you're gonna recoil, just a little."

"What?" she smiled.

"Like this." He laid a palm over her forearm and, almost automatically she responded by calmly drawing her arm away. Lefty kept his eye in the mirror. "Perfect. Oh he totally saw that. OK." Lefty reached in his breast pocket and drew out a pen. He stretched across the bar and grabbed a bar napkin. "I'm pretending to ask for your number. And you're not going to do it."

"How long have you been insane?"

"Just smile and shake your head no."

She smiled and gently shook her head.

He appeared to be pleading with her. "Good, once more."

She did it again.

Lefty gave his shoulders a little shrug. "OK. Now when he comes over, tell him I asked for your number, but you said you don't just give it out to random guys."

"Well at least that's true."

"Good. Cause he's gonna wanna believe it too." He reached out to shake her hand and she instinctually took it. "Good luck. Seriously."

"Thanks, Lefty."

"Invite me to the wedding."

She smiled softly as Lefty stepped into the rush of bar music, toward the front door and began walking, three blocks toward home. After locking the door of his flat behind him he fed his two goldfish, Rachel and Brian, then reached for the TV remote. He paused, then reached for a framed photograph of a woman. A funeral card was tucked in the corner of the frame.

"The office was never the same after you," he said.

He set the frame back in its place and flipped on the TV. A few blocks away, a woman flipped her hair and smiled as a co-worker finally decided to ask what she was doing this weekend.

29

Strays

by Kyle Hemmings

Martha, at fifty-one years, a mature lust of a woman – got laid. She got laid by someone she hardly knew at The Norwegian Wood. He claimed he had ridden with a dangerous motorcycle gang, The Backdoor Huns. At one time, he said, they owned Ventura Highway. Martha blinked twice and said she read about them somewhere.

She gave him a ride to her place on her motorcycle.

After he left, after he finished the last batch of her pancakes, Martha wanted to shout to the world, to all her married friends living inside barren broom closets – I GOT LAID, BITCHES! Martha felt sexy at the law office. She spread her legs while typing up her boss's raspy dictations.

She was even tempted to share the news with her tailless Manx cat – Mr. Stubbin. At night, he slept curled at her feet. She suspected there was something telepathic in his eyes. She thought he could read her.

So when Martha called the ex-biker and warrior love-maker, she kept hearing, "This number is no longer in service."

But she didn't give up hope. After all, she got laid, didn't she?

That is, until she visited her gynecologist, an older woman addicted to Nicorette gum who had a noticeable twitch.

"You have genital herpes. I think you should contact your sex partners."

"Sex partners? Where? Okay. I had unprotected sex with this guy who was so hung ... I mean who I hung around with one night. I mean we hung together."

After the doctor handed her some tissues, Martha wiped her eyes and mumbled, "'STD.' It stands for Stupid Transgressions for Dummies like me."

At home, she cried into Mr. Stubbin's fur. His eyes seemed to say: Give me water. There are other needs than yours.

She said to Mr. Stubbin, I will be alone for the rest of my life.

But wasn't it a good lay? Mr. Stubbin might have said.

Martha went back to The Norwegian Wood. She drank Bahama Mamas and Anejo Highballs until she could no longer focus on her runny make-up in the mirror, herpes, or the dreadful possibility of abstaining from sex.

She met a cute guy with tapering chin, pug nose, and dimples punctuating either side of his smile. He was younger than she by at least two decades. He impressed her with his zest, with his take on old colloquialisms, such as There's more than one way to slick a cat.

"How the hell did you know I have a cat?" she said.

"I didn't," he said. He burped and excused himself. "I forgot my damn apartment keys."

"It's okay. I'll give you a ride to my place. Hope motorcycles don't make you sick."

They stopped at an all-night diner and ordered cups of black coffee and charcoal-burnt cheeseburgers with fat grease-dripping fries. As she sobered, she felt the eyes of a husky truck driver upon her.

"Let's go," she said to cute guy. "I got the bill."

"I haven't finished my second burger."

"You'll probably retch it up later. C'mon."

She put him up in her extra bed.

His eyes grew big and scared. He flinched. His jet black hair, which had been combed straight back, was now messed up, flopping over his forehead.

She was tempted to jump in next to him, make out, expose half of her bad boys, her mother's euphemism for breasts.

The cute guy sat up in bed and managed a tense smile.

"Can I touch you? Sometimes when I touch someone, it makes me less nervous. You have a really nice face," he said.

"Yes," she said, "but just a quick touch. No foreplay."

He tried to touch her cheek, but his hand quivered, then flopped back on the bed. "Did anyone ever tell you that you have a nice face?"

Martha shook her head. She pursed her lips like a little girl about to confess a secret. "I've been told I have a handsome face. Great compliment, isn't it?"

He smiled at her. Something inside her tingled.

Martha's lower lip trembled and her eyes welled up. He sat up and held out his arms. She refused to budge and sobbed, "I just can't! I can't fuck you because I have this rare form of SOMETHING, and it makes me itch at the wrong time in the wrong place. They got me on three different medications and I still itch like a girl scout after a night of sleeping near poison oak and dreaming of Justin Bieber."

"It's okay," he said, "I'm gay."

She sniffed again. She couldn't decide whether she should slap him or love him.

30

The Life of a Pretty Girl

by Jennifer Chardon

"What's it like?" he asks, tilting his head to one side, "the life of a pretty girl?"

I like the way he says pretty. Prit. Tee. It's a stupid thing to say but he owns it in that accent, smirking into his beer.

"Oh, it's fucking dandy," I say, matching his grin.

"She's a sharp one," he laughs and we clink our glasses together as if it's our thing and we hadn't just met a couple of hours ago. His hand finds my knee underneath the tiny table. I sip my wine, glad I didn't take a pill this morning. The meds make me slow. I'm so much better without them on my dates.

"I quite like you," he says, almost merging the words together, like he can't get them out fast enough. But he's right on time. I draw a second date box for him in my head.

I chose Tom the way I choose them all. The ones who seem to have the least in common with me. Tom's profile says he travels a lot, works in publishing. He lists Himalayan salt as something he can't live without.

"Likewise," I say and he squeezes my knee. A lot of them are too scared to touch so soon. He smiles again and grazes his fingers against my powdered pink cheek. It's too early to kiss me though. I hope he knows that.

He does. He moves his hand away to pick up and finish the rest of his beer. "You want another?" he asks, nodding to my half empty glass.

"Definitely." I down the rest of my wine. "It's my round though," I say as I make a mock show of reaching for my purse.

"No chance," he says, taking his other hand from my knee and heading to the bar.

I never buy the drinks but I always make the same show. I note the reactions.

The bar he's chosen is cave-like and dark, tea-light candles make the tiny space glow. It's the kind of light that flatters everyone. There are mirrors everywhere, making it hard for me not to stare at myself. My eyes seem brighter behind charcoal eyeliner, healthier. Before my dates I always spend half an hour in Sephora, wandering around the store coating layers of samples on my face. I can't get ready in my bathroom. I prefer strangers seeing me put on lipstick.

I watch Tom at the bar, casually chatting to the guy waiting beside him. I want to feel bad for Tom but he's indistinguishable to me already, just someone else to key in.

My therapist told me this is normal. The medication is supposed to help me keep my emotions proportionate to the situation. She recently suggested I consider quitting The Spreadsheet.

I consider what I will write in Tom's first box.

I started The Spreadsheet a year ago when I found myself on a third date. In the middle of my mozzarella salad appetizer I realized I'd forgotten everything about the guy I was sitting across from. I couldn't even recall where we'd had our last date the week before.

The thought of giving up The Spreadsheet makes my pulse move into my throat, like I'll choke on my pounding heart. My therapist said this is the reason we're here.

"Here we are," Tom says, putting down a glass of Sancerre on the tiny table between us.

"I really never do this online dating thing," he says, sipping from a tumbler, something dark brown and neat.

"Never?" They all find a way to say the same thing.

"Well, not often."

"Ever meet anyone special?" I ask, staring at the tiny candle between us. This is one of my key questions, a special side-note on my sheet.

"Now I have," he winks in a cute-not-creepy way. It's a good answer.

"Have you?"

"I'm starting to think so," I say. My standard good answer.

"You really are pretty." Prit. Tee. I realize I'm almost drunk. It's that time of night. I take a big gulp of wine. "Childhood."

"Yeah?" Tom looks at me carefully.

"How was yours?" I'm ready for the big reveal, the reason I keep doing this.

"It was pretty ordinary," Tom says shrugging. Prit. Tee. Another good answer from Tom.

"Yours?" he asks.

"My Mom used to put bits of electrical tape all over our bathroom tiles. She thought we were being watched."

I don't blame my mother anymore, I understand now she was sick. My therapist calls this progress.

"I'm so sorry," he says, pulling me to him. I breathe in his scent of expensive man perfume and Glenmorangie. In my head I delete the two extra boxes beside his name.

31

The Tam

by Karen Eileen Sikola

Madeline started going to The Tam because it was cheap, and because it reminded her of Manny's Tam O'Shanter, where she first ate quail in a dress too informal for junior prom.

At first, she went with coworkers, to celebrate birthdays, publications, or getting the hell out of there. Then she started going alone, telling herself It made more sense to spend three dollars on a pint of Amber Bock than a shot of espresso at the Thinking Cup down the street.

Before moving to Boston, Madeline had a hometown watering hole, where nobody knew her name, but everyone knew her drink. Malibu Diet, they called her.

When the weather was nice, and even when it wasn't, she and Andy would sit outside so he could smoke. If there were no empty tables on the patio, Madeline would hold down fort in a corner booth. While Andy smoked outside, she'd continue pouring mini bottles of Cooks into smudged flutes just to keep her hands busy.

It seemed acceptable to drink one's way through grad school. Madeline and Andy met their professors at bars and called it office hours. They met their friends at bars and called it lunch.

When Andy chose San Francisco over finishing his thesis, Madeline understood. He had to go. He had to see the world in order to write about it. He had to live somewhere he felt accepted more than one night a week at a cowboy bar-turned dance club. He had to go where the gin was two for one.

Perhaps The Tam reminded her of home. Perhaps cheap booze reminded her of friendship.

32

One More Round

by Diana J. Wynne

He texts that he's leaving, so I head for Lone Palm, the vaguely art deco bar that's halfway between us. It's not perfect, but good enough on a Thursday. Well, martinis and Cosmos, bowls of wasabi peas on white tablecloths. And not too many of the kids we blame for ruining the Mission, even though not so long ago we were those kids.

I pass the Google bus letting off passengers. A curly-haired guy talking on his phone takes a unicycle off the bike rack, climbs on, and rides off, all without a break in the conversation.

When I first moved here, a college friend lived next to Lone Palm. I stopped by for brunch on the way to a street fair. We sat on plastic crates in an empty Victorian. His roommates poured coffee from a French press and proudly passed around a binder of before-and-after pictures of gleaming hardwood floors. I was 23 and lived in a room not much bigger than my double bed. I made $16,000 a year; they'd probably spent that much on cabinets.

David had the touch. Any neighborhood he lived in quickly went from sketchy to chic. A savvier businessperson would have followed him around investing. I was too busy falling in love to capitalize, building things that were going to change the world.

Tonight we're talking about pitching start-ups and where to go July 4th and whether we'll ever leave our tiny rent-controlled apartments. (Probably not.) Like every generation that comes to the city, we're scornful of new arrivals, who run up prices for real estate and burritos while forgetting the companies we founded and subsequently ran into the ground. They seem less passionate about technology, more interested in getting rich, or so we tell ourselves.

By now we've moved a few blocks to a place on 24th that serves poutine. We're not impressed. There's a bar where drinks are named for novelists and another where they're "inspired" by Pantone colors. But there's a line to get in, so we go to Homestead. Tall guys in ski sweaters down pints of Guinness and throw peanut shells on the floor.

He gets impatient if the bartenders take too long mixing "artisanal" cocktails with housemade bitters, making milkshakes with Scotch. He grew up over a pub his family owned. They'll be out of business in five months, he predicts, maybe four. Usually he's right.

You can spot the trust fund kids a mile off, the ones who don't really need a job muddling mojitos. Owning a bar is the new winery or coffee roastery. It's what you do after your start-up is bought by Facebook or Yahoo, and you need a break to recalibrate your life.

(I roast gray-green Arabica beans in a fry pan and shake the dust from the skins off the edge of my fire escape. It's fun to geek out over water temperature and achieving the perfect crema. My Aeropress is a better French press, designed by the folks in Palo Alto who make Aerobie, the aerodynamic Frisbee. The Bay Area is about nothing if not upgrades and continuous cycles of boom and bust, and reinvention.)

We plot our game plan on a cocktail napkin and share French fries topped with beef marrow (practically a superfood, he assures me). He used to smoke, and I'd flirt idly with the bartender while he paced outside and talked on the phone to a friend in the middle of a breakup or family someplace it was hours later.

Later we'll wind up at Doc's or the Attic or Phone Booth for a nightcap, places you only go after midnight, when the last BART train has left the station, when your makeup's half-melted or you're looking for someone to take home. By now we're low on cash. Long ago, he taught me never to run a tab or drink on plastic, a rule that's served me well.

There's no absinthe or elderflower liqueur or fancy bottles of tonic. Bars like this will still be here next year, even if some of the people in them will have moved on in search of the next big thing.

I stagger to the day-glo bathroom to see how my mascara's holding up. A frizzy-haired raccoon stares back. Prince is playing on the jukebox. I spy a familiar face. "Omigod, Diana Wynne!" Scott cries. "What are *you* doing here?"

I make my way to a seat in the corner against the wall, and he leans in to describe what I've missed. I feel his warm breath on my neck as I sip my nightcap.

He has to get up early for a flight to NY, so we finish up and head out. He walks me partway, past the imaginary dividing line of rival gangs and kisses me lightly on the lips, one more last call in the town we call home.

authors

Christopher Allen (*The Man Who Can't be Moved*), a native Tennessean, lives in Germany. He's the author of *Conversations with S. Teri O'Type (a Satire)*, an episodic adult cartoon about a man struggling with expectations. A past *Glimmer Train* finalist, Allen has been nominated for Best of the Net as well as the Pushcart Prize twice. He blogs about his absurd need to see the entire planet at htt://www.imustbeoff.com.

Claudia Bierschenk's (*Coffin Showroom*) poetry has been published in *Juice Press*, *Full of Crow*, *Public Republic*, *Alittlepoetry*, *Durable Goods*, and *SAND Journal*. Her first poetry chapbook *Perestroika Silence* was published by erbacce Press, Liverpool in spring 2010, and her work has also featured in several poetry anthologies by ForwardPress, Peterborough (UK). Claudia has been previously nominated for the Pushcart Poetry Prize and for Best of the Net. She won 3rd place at the 2011 Berlin Poetry Awards. Claudia lives in Berlin.

Arthur Carey (*Last Call at the Do Drop Inn*) is a former newspaper reporter and journalism instructor who lives in the San Francisco Bay area. He is a member of the California Writers Club. His fiction has appeared in print and internet publications, including *Pedestal Magazine*, *Funny Times*, *Eclectic Flash*, *Writers' Journal*, *Golden Visions Magazine*, *Suspense*, *Abstract Quill*, *Clever Magazine* and *Still Crazy*. He is the author of *The Gender War*, a humor novel.

Jennifer Chardon (*The Life of a Pretty Girl*) is a writer with secret dreams of also becoming a comedian and / or hairdresser. She is currently at work on her first novel, *Chasing Summer*. The title will probably change. She has spent much of the last five years backpacking, journal writing and staying up late. Her last one-way ticket brought her to New York City where she now finds herself refusing to leave. Find her on Twitter @jenniferchardon or visit her website at http://www.jenniferchardon.com.

Ramon Collins (*Waiting with Merle*) lives on the NE edge of the Mojave Desert with an Irish wife and two Animal Rescue dogs. He's had several stories published and even more posted online.

Paul Combs (*Union Jack*) is a writer and bookseller living in North Texas. His ultimate goal (besides playing bass in the E Street Band or goalkeeper for FC Barcelona) is to make reading, writing, and books in general as popular in Texas as high school football. It may take him a while. You can find his book reviews and thoughts on books and bookselling at http://somersetbooks.blogspot.com/.

Norman Conquest (*A Man Walks into a Barcode*) is a verbo-visual artist based in the Bay Area, His most recent book, *WHAT IS ART?*, was published by JEF Books, and he is the Président-Fondateur of Black Scat Books.

Christine Cook (*Hollywood Cemetery*) is about to graduate from Seattle Pacific University where she has spent the last three years learning to write creatively and trying to avoid perky people. She is from the Pacific Northwest, subscribing to typical Seattle obsessions: indie rock, coffee, and black clothing. She works behind the scenes in the independent music industry, which gives her ample writing inspiration and a wry sense of humor.

Joanna Delooze (*Gullible*) is an ex-pat New Yorker living in Northwest England with her very English husband and two all-singing, all-dancing, all-skateboarding, artsy teenage boys. She writes to get the voices out of her head and onto the page. (It's rather crowded up there!) You can read her blog at http://bumblefingers.blogspot.co.uk/ and follow her on Twitter @josiejo127.

Shane Frazier (*WTF?*), originally from the shores of the Left Side of the States (Southern California), can be found living in Las Vegas, Nevada, where he does nothing but sit by in his pool, drink Tuaca with his wife, and bitch about his five children (along with three grandchildren). He is currently in mourning for his fish, Lopez, who passed suddenly after a long battle with substance-abuse.

S. H. Gall (*Holiday*) writes flash fiction, and occasionally non-fiction. His work can be found in such diverse markets as *SmokeLong Quarterly*, *Metazen*, *decomP MagazinE*, *Monkeybicycle*, and *fwriction : review*, to name a few. His work can be found online and in print from *Pure Slush*.

Gloria Garfunkel (*Sobriety Group*) is the daughter of two Auschwitz survivors and has a Ph.D. in Psychology from Harvard. Her short stories and flash fiction have appeared in over 30 literary journals.

Walter Giersbach (*Sammy the Madman's Near Death Experience*) has had fiction appear in *Bewildering Stories*, *Big Pulp*, *Corner Club Press*, *Every Day Fiction*, *Gumshoe Review*, *OG Short Fiction*, *Over My Dead Body*, *Pif Magazine*, *Pulp Modern*, *r.kv.r.y*, *Short Fiction World*, *The World of Myth*, and a dozen other publications. He also writes on military history and social phenomena. Two volumes of short stories, *Cruising the Green of Second Avenue*, are available at Barnes & Noble and other online booksellers. You can find his blog at http://allotropiclucubrations.blogspot.com/.

Teresa Burns Gunther (*Plonk*) has had fiction and nonfiction appear in numerous literary journals and most recently in *Northwind Magazine*, obit. *Pure Slush Vol. 6*, *Bookslut* and *Best New Writing 2012*. Teresa is the Editor of *The Lakeside*, an on-line literary magazine, and she founded *Lakeshore Writers Workshop* in Oakland, California where she leads creative writing workshops and classes and works one-on-one with writers. You can find her and links to her work at http://www.teresaburnsgunther.com/.

Kyle Hemmings (*Strays*) is the author of several chapbooks of poetry and prose: *Avenue C, Cat People, Anime Junkie* (Scars Publications), *Void & Sky* (Outskirts Press) and *Tokyo Girls in Science Fiction* (NAP). He has been published in *elimae, Smokelong Quarterly, Match Book, Wigleaf*, and elsewhere. He loves cats, dogs, and 60's garage bands.

After retiring in 2009, it took **Joanne Jagoda** (*Mac's Place*), one inspiring writing workshop to begin a long-postponed creative writing journey. Since discovering her passion for writing, she has been working on short stories, poetry and non-fiction. Her work has been published in e-zines and print anthologies including *Pure Slush* online, *52 / 250 A Year of Flash, Adventures for Women, Poetica*, and *Still Crazy*. She lives in Oakland, California and is the short story editor for *Poetica*, continues taking writing workshops and classes in the Bay Area, enjoys Zumba, traveling with her husband and visiting her three grandchildren in Jerusalem who call her *Savta*.

Joyce Juzwik (*Happy Anniversary*) has a crime fiction novel, *King's Bishop Takes King's Rook's Pawn*, and a six-part children's fantasy series, *Choices*, published by DiskUs Publishing; a horror short published in the anthology *Deathgrip: The Legacy*; short stories published in the charity anthology *Lost Children*, and in the *Pure Slush* print anthologies *Notausgang: emergency exit, obit.,* and *gorge*. Her crime fiction / noir stories have appeared in *A Twist of Noir, Pulp Metal Magazine, Powder Burn Flash, Shotgun Honey*, and *Pure Slush* online. She always has a novel and story or two in the works, and she blogs at http://jfjuzwik.blogspot.com/

Len Kuntz (*Parasites* and *Boxers*) is a writer from Washington State and an editor at the online literary magazine *Metazen*. His work appears widely in print and online. You can find him at http://lenkuntz.blogspot.com.

Matt McGee's (*True Shock* and *Lefty, Daisy and the Clueless Man*) *True Shock* is based on real events and a true lifestyle. To those widowed, murdered, broken-hearted by those living for the perpetuation of their own good time in The Tunnel: live on. And to the Golden Children who do whatever it takes: "Before the inferno, my heart was light."

Matt Potter (*Capitalist Bastard*) is an Australian-born writer who keeps a part of his psyche in Berlin. Matt has been published in various places online, and he is, rather amazingly, also the founding editor of *Pure Slush*. Find more of his work at http://mattcpotter.webs.com/.

Misti Rainwater-Lites (*Miracles*) is the author of several collections of poetry and fiction. *Bullshit Rodeo*, a novel, is forthcoming from Epic Rites Press in July 2013. Find Misti's blog here: http://dondeestaeldiscochupacabra.blogspot.com.

Martha Rand (*Sloe Gin Fizz is Pink*) writes and paints in New Jersey. She learned to juggle at a Renaissance Faire and has used this skill consistently ever since to live her life as fully as possible. Once upon a time she was the talent on a yoga TV show for kids which led to meeting her current husband of 27 years who really does work for TV news. Her favorite flowers are violets and currently she is in love with chunky guacamole and corn on the cob with cilantro herb butter.

Stephen V. Ramey (*Another Saturday Night*) is an American author from New Castle, Pennsylvania. His work has appeared in many places, including *The Doctor TJ Eckleburg Review*, *The Journal of Compressed Creative Arts*, and *A Capella Zoo*. *Glass Animals*, his first collection of (very) short fiction is available from *Pure Slush Books*. Find him and more of his work at http://www.stephenvramey.com.

Desmond Shortt (*Beaver Lodge*) Ever since a childhood shopping trip, when he walked into a glass door while trying out a pair of shoes, Desmond Shortt has remained suspicious of transparency.

Beate Sigriddaughter (*Cabeceo*) lives and writes in North Vancouver, Canada. Her work has received three Pushcart Prize nominations. She has also established the Glass Woman Prize to honor passionate women's voices. Her published work includes the pro-peace novel *Parcival* and a collection of philosophical flash fiction entitled *The Unicorn And ...* . Find her website here: http://www.sigriddaughter.com

Karen Eileen Sikola (*The Tam*) received her M.F.A. in Creative Nonfiction from California State University, Fresno in 2009. She now lives in Boston, where she works in publishing and plays mommy to two pound puppies, Rilo and Watson. Her writing has appeared in several online journals, including *Monkeybicycle*, *Ploughshares*, and *fwriction : review*. Her chapbook, *Riding the Green Line*, is available for download from Walleyed Press.

Andrew J Stone (*First Time*) currently attends Seattle Pacific University where he spends $40,000 a year to learn how to lie more intelligently. He originally hails from Los Angeles but moved to Seattle to avoid the damned sun. His debut chapbook, *Teenage Angst & the Ekphrastic Exercise*, will be available from Collective Banter Press sometime in 2013. Other work has been discovered in *Hobart*, *Marco Polo*, and *Red Fez*. He dwells in the graveyard here: http://andrewjstone.blogspot.com/.

Ben Tanzer (*So Different Now*) is an Emmy Award-winning Public Service Announcement writer and the author of the books *My Father's House, You Can Make Him Like You, So Different Now*, and the forthcoming *Orphans and Lost in Space*, among others. Ben is also the Editor of the anthology *Daddy Cool*, oversees day-to-day operations of *This Zine Will Change Your Life* and can be found online at *This Blog Will Change Your Life*, the center of his growing lifestyle empire.

Alun Williams (*One Night at Harry's*) also writes under the names Maxwell Allen and Maxieslim, on forums such as Zoetrope and Critters-bar. He resides in Wales but lives in his head above a seedy bar in downtown LA with Philip Marlowe and Charles Bukowski. He has no blog or website yet. He has previously been published in *Pure Slush* online, *Boyslut, Yellow Mama* and *Do Hookers Kiss*, and states, "If I wrote for money, I'd starve to death!"

Diana J. Wynne (*One More Round*), when she's not roasting coffee or making bathtub gin, designs software. Her stories have appeared in *The New York Times*, *Salon*, *Mississippi Review*, *The Raw Story*, and *Pure Slush* online and in print. Every hour can be happy hour.

Acknowledgements

An earlier version of *So Different Now* by **Ben Tanzer** was previously published in *Dogplotz* and the print collection *So Different Now*.

An earlier version of *Last Call at the Do Drop Inn* by **Arthur Carey** was previously published in *Pedestal Magazine*.

Claudia Bierschenk thanks Desmond Shortt and Matt Potter for their helpful comments on *Coffin Showroom*.

Other books from *Pure Slush*

For the complete range of *Pure Slush*
anthologies and single author books,
visit the *Pure Slush* Store
http://pureslush.webs.com/store.htm

Catherine refracted
Pure Slush Vol. 7
ISBN: 978-1-304-12272-8
Catherine the Great, Empress and
Autocrat of All the Russias, was a
fascinating woman and legends about
her abound.

Catherine refracted is a re-imagining of
the life and the legends of Catherine the
Great. Her lovers, her illegitimate
children, her wiles, her wit and her place in history ... all
feature in this lively reinterpretation of one of history's most
beloved and reviled leaders.

Featuring the work of nineteen writers, including rare juvenilia
and modern reappraisals of Catherine the Great's place in
world cultural history.

Originally published June 2013

obit. Pure Slush Vol. 6

ISBN: 978-1-300-86001-3

Webster Murphy Allen 1925 – 2012.
Lawyer, opera-goer, philanthropist, father, grandfather, generous with his time and talents and money ... or was he?

obit. explores the many sides of a man many people *thought* they knew. Each writer has taken an incident or anecdote or memory from Webster's life and created a fully-fleshed man with multiple quirks ... and multiple secrets.

Where does the truth lie? Featuring 32 different takes on Webster Murphy Allen's life by 22 different writers.

Originally published March 2013

Versus. Pure Slush Vol. 5

ISBN: 978-1-300-76169-3

Can good poetry be written on demand? The answer is "Yes" and *Versus* is the proof.　　　*Bill Yarrow*

5 poets write 15 poems each against 15 different topics, the collection featuring 75 different opinions. All are different and unique in their own way.

These 5 poets are each unique in their approach and style yet they seem to coalesce, the way a single puddle can be splashed with a variety of colors.　　　*Susan Tepper*

Originally published February 2013

gorge

Pure Slush Vol. 4

a novel in stories

gorge: a novel in stories
Pure Slush Vol. 4

ISBN: 978-1-300-54979-6

54 stories told by 33 writers. Each story is a chapter in the tale of the misplaced Café Gano, a restaurant in a small town on the Maine coast. The action takes place over one day, and as the afternoon progresses and the evening unfolds, customers' lives unravel and staff decorum snaps to erupt in a crescendo of miscalculated faith and desperate bids for ultimate control. Yeah, it's that crazy!!

For any person who has ever worked in a restaurant, or been a patron, you will laugh aloud at the follies, wonder who will hook up with whom, and at the pace I read this, ask yourself, when will *Pure Slush* bring out the next novel of compilations?

Robert Vaughan

Recommended, particularly if you appreciate a bold experiment in narrative and variety of perspective.

Stephen V. Ramey
Originally published December 2012

real Pure Slush Vol. 3

ISBN: 978-1-291-14109-2

upfront! uptight! up-yours! Cutting edge non-fiction from thirty-one writers who spill their guts on life and love, sex and travel, food and legalities and freedom and family and reflect the true diversity of everyday experience.

Originally published October 2012

real

Pure Slush Vol. 3

Notausgang: emergency exit
Pure Slush Vol. 2
ISBN: 978-1-4717-0059-0
Stories desperate and amusing, based on the theme *emergency exit*. (*Notausgang* is German for *emergency exit*.) Scary, creepy, funny, illuminating, sad and life-affirming. Twenty-four stories, fiction and non-fiction.

Every story in this collection, while based on the same theme, is well-crafted, rich in the detail of countless settings, and full of interesting and unique characters, each with their own journey through life, with all its unpredictable twists and turns. All the stories are short ones, yet each contains their characters' lifetimes and then some – each seeking some type of 'emergency exit' in their own way.

Joyce Juzwik
Originally published May 2012

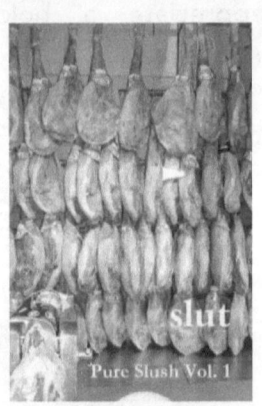

slut Pure Slush Vol. 1
(2nd edition)
ISBN: 978-1-4716-0674-8
a zesty, amusing (and serious) anthology of fiction and non-fiction on the theme 'slut' ... where it all began!!

Originally published February 2012

For the complete range of *Pure Slush* books and eBooks, visit the *Pure Slush* Store at http://pureslush.webs.com/store.htm

www.ingramcontent.com/pod-product-compliance
Lightning Source LLC
Chambersburg PA
CBHW050828180626
46814CB00004B/1506